IMPERFECT

W WINTERS

AUTHOR'S COPYRIGHT

SYNOPSIS

From *USA Today* bestselling author W Winters comes an emotionally gripping romantic suspense.

It's been a long time since I've looked at a man and wanted something more.

Even longer since one has looked at me with a gaze that I couldn't tear my eyes from.

One look and I was tempted; one taste and I was addicted.

No one is perfect, but that's how it felt to be in his arms.

I started to think everything was going to be alright. That life had finally put the pieces of my broken heart back together.

Fate may have brought us together, it's a pretty little thought my poetic mind had.

But there's no doubt that the sins of his past would tear us apart.

"Reading this book leaves you with raw feelings and can break

your heart. A very intense love story packed in one single book."
Andrea, early review

"Love is more than words; my heart can tell you that." - DLS
To Donna, always an inspiration.

PROLOGUE

on't let them see.

Her words echo in my head as I stalk toward the quiet bedroom. She whispered them against my lips last night. The cool air slipped between us as she broke our kiss and slowly opened her eyes in the dark of the night.

The street light shined down around us on the back porch of her place on the Upper East Side. The city life slept quietly so late at night, or early in the morning, depending on how you look at it. Only the sinners like us were left awake.

Don't let them see. She left me with the parting plea and here I am… giving into her wish.

I've never crept through anyone's back door so late at night. Not once in my life have I had to sneak around like this.

I don't want to keep doing this shit, but here I am. What the hell has this woman done to me? *I'm wrapped around her little finger.*

It's because she's ashamed. I know that's why she doesn't want people to know we're together. Not just a fling, not a rebound fuck. There's something more to us now, but she doesn't want the world to know.

1

The floorboards creak under my weight and I hesitate in the doorway, the dim lamp from the hall filling the dark room with a hint of light. It's her place and her neighbors aren't going to hear, but I don't want to disturb her.

It's obvious she's sleeping, but she stirs beneath the silk duvet until finally she opens her eyes and sees me. She tilts her head to the side as she looks at me, burying her cheek into the pillow, a soft smile playing on her lips.

"I missed you," she says and her voice is laced with an equal mix of sleep and lust.

If only she knew the real reason I crave her touch. The reason I'm so tempted to break all my rules.

"I'm sorry I'm late," I tell her in a deep, rough voice as I start unbuttoning my shirt. A smirk turns the corners of my lips up as her eyes sparkle with humor. She doesn't care when I come and go, so long as I lie in her bed at night, or she in mine.

Her doe eyes stare back at me while I slip off the button up and let it pool into a puddle at my feet. I yank my tight white undershirt over my head and look back to see those lush lips parted.

She likes what she sees. My muscles ripple as I let the tank drop to the floor, the moonlight bathing the room and the two of us in a faint glow.

She may want to keep this a secret, but she fucking wants me and she can't hide it. I've become addicted to the way she looks at me like she needs to touch me to stay grounded, just as she needs to breathe air to survive. I've learned to crave the faint sounds of her quickened breath as she waits for me to come to her. *As if she'd die without me.*

I'm slow to unbuckle my belt as my eyes roam down her curves. She's mine to take. Mine to touch. *Mine to keep.*

If it were up to me, I'd take her ass outside and into the middle of the busy city street to show the world that she belongs to me now. I don't want to sneak around anymore and I don't give a shit who knows. I'm tired of this bullshit.

The anger boils in my blood as I grip my leather belt tighter, making it sing in the air as I pull it through the loops and drop it to the floor with a loud clack. All the while my gaze is on her gorgeous eyes, and she's staring back at me with the same desire as I have for her.

The past is over and done. No one will ever know what really happened -- not her, not anyone.

"Mason," she practically whimpers my name and it pulls the beast in me closer to her. My knee dips into the bed, making it groan with my weight as I crawl over to her.

Her soft blue eyes pierce through me, cutting through the dark room. More of the soft lighting from the city slips into the room as the heat kicks on and the curtains sway. The way the light kisses her skin as she pushes the duvet away makes her all the more beautiful.

She's laid out for me. *All for me.* She fucking needs me.

I crush my lips to hers and dig my fingers into the flesh of her hips as she spreads her thighs for me. Her soft moans fill the hot air between us.

She's ashamed to be moving on so quickly. Especially with a man like me. I wasn't made for a woman like her. I'm someone who could tarnish her sterling reputation and make the crack in her picture-perfect frame splinter even deeper. To say I'm rough around the edges is putting it lightly, but I have what it takes to keep her.

We both know this was supposed to be a one-time thing. But now, I want more.

She thinks she's ruined, but she's fucking perfect. It's my sins and my secrets that could destroy us both. I'll never let them come to light. Not now that I have something worth fighting for.

She doesn't know it yet, but I won't stop until she's mine.

She needs to get over it and just accept this for what it is. She's fucking mine now.

CHAPTER 1

Mason

Sinful pasts will haunt us both.
They never leave, they stay like ghosts.
You can't outrun them.
You can't hide.
When they come back to life,
They'll all know you lied.

"YOU SHOULD BE THANKING me for covering up your mess," my father says from his high-back desk chair. His fingers grip the leather arms and the tips of his thumbs rub gently back and forth across the brass studs.

Though the blinds are closed, the tall windows behind my father fill the large office with the dim light from the evening sun.

I look over my shoulder at him, still holding a random law

textbook I've taken from the floor-to-ceiling shelves that line the side walls of his office. The room smells of old books. With the dark wood, tan leather and deep red Beaumont rug, the decor reeks of old money and that's exactly what this room represents.

That and bullshit.

Lies and corruption are what have held this room in its current state for generations. I've pretended for so long that it wasn't true. But learning about what my father's done... I can't turn a blind eye to it anymore. It's undeniable and unforgivable.

I huff a small laugh, not letting him see how affected I am. "For the last time," I tell him as I shut the book and smirk at him, "it wasn't my mess."

I'm not admitting to shit. Not even to my own father. In this city, one slip up could send you tumbling into an early grave. Like my mother and like the mess my father's referring to. I don't trust him. I don't trust anyone any longer.

My father's eyes turn to slits as his face reddens before picking up the cup of hot coffee. He holds the black mug with both of his hands, blowing across the top and refusing to acknowledge me.

"You would have gone through hell-"

I cut my father off, although my voice doesn't reflect any emotion whatsoever. It's a turning point in our relationship. Instead of him getting me worked up, it's the opposite. "No I wouldn't have." I look him in the eyes as I add, "I would have been just fine."

A moment passes and the only sound is the ticking of the large clock on the right side of the room. "It wasn't my mess you cleaned up, and we both know it." He's the first to look away, but instead of showing remorse, he only looks pissed.

"Did you need anything else?" I ask him. I just want to get the fuck out of here and back to the construction site. This office reminds me of my grandfather, a man I loved and trusted. But he was a man who turned out to be just like all the rest of the powerful men in this city. Ruled by sin.

"I'm tired of you getting into trouble," he finally says. He's lost his fucking mind. This is the first time in my life I've truly been in control of myself. No more fucking around. The recent events have been sobering. When I was a hormone-filled teen dealing with grief and anger, it was easy to pick fights. First, the death of my grandfather and then my mother. It was easy to act out.

Thirty-three is too fucking old for that bullshit. I finally have my life together... all but the ties to my father. It's a tangled mess of lies and money. Much like everyone else's dealings in this city.

The thought makes my eyes fall to the floor and then look back up to the shelves to mindlessly scan the spines of the ancient texts.

Knowing what my father did makes all those memories of losing my mother surface. My stomach churns and my blood heats as adrenaline courses through me, adrenaline pushing me to confront the man I no longer know.

I clench my hand into a fist and bring it to my mouth as I clear my throat and take a few steps towards him. He's the one who called this meeting, demanded it really. But he hasn't even risen from his chair. Lazy fucker.

"I don't know what you're talking about," I answer him easily. "I haven't got a single problem on my mind." I give him a polite smile and keep the charming look on my face. It only makes him angrier and I fucking love every second of his pissed-off expression. He thought I'd feel as if I owed him.

But I don't owe him shit.

I may be just like him in looks. Tall, dark and handsome, or so they say. A brilliant smile with an air of ease that's made to fool and seduce the best of them. It makes sense that he's a lawyer. Really it's a family business really, but if it wasn't, it'd still be the profession most apt for my father.

"You need to quit this shit and do what you're told, Mason." My father stands from his seat quickly, his chair rolling backward and smacking against the wall. It hits the blinds and streams of light flicker into the room.

"I don't need to do shit." He could talk to me like that all he wanted back when I was a child or before I knew the truth, but now I have no respect for the man in front of me. I'm disgusted by him and caught on the edge of what's right and wrong. I should turn him in and let him rot in jail. I grit my teeth as I stare back at him. It's what's right, but I can't bring myself to send my own father to prison.

A low hum of admonishment deep in his throat makes the smirk on my face widen into a smile.

"I have my own company, my own life-" I start but my father cuts me off. Nothing new there.

"You were born a Thatcher, and you'll die a Thatcher." The words leave a chill across my skin. That's the core of the problem. I was born into this shit and I can't run from it. And my company is in debt to him. It was a rookie mistake I made before I knew what I was doing. Back when I didn't see him for the man he really is.

"Why do you even give a fuck?" I finally ask him. His pristine reputation is just fine now that I'm an adult and I've moved on from the fuck-up I used to be. "I'm not the one coming to you-"

"*She* did," he answers simply, with a spark in his eyes and the corners of his lips upturned as if that's all the ammunition he needs. And in some respects, he's right. They all know where I come from. They know I have money and power behind me. And that's all anyone in this city cares about anyway.

I shrug my shoulders and walk closer to the desk, bracing myself by gripping the back of the chair opposite him. "You decided to deal with her when what she said was a lie." I stare him in the eyes, willing him to tell me again how he *saved* me. It's complete bullshit. "She didn't have shit on me. She couldn't have done anything!" My voice rises and I hate that I've shown him this weak side of me.

Control. I thrive with control.

A heavy breath leaves him as he gazes back with pure hate but he doesn't say a word. I knew he wouldn't. He's wrong. Dead fucking wrong and utterly ruined if I open my mouth to anyone. He did it so I'd owe him, but in reality we both know that he owes me now.

"It's your fuck up, not mine." I practically spit out the words and shove the chair forward as I turn to leave him. My body's tense and the anger is increasing. I try not to let it show. I fucking hate that I can't control myself around this prick. Everyone else I can handle, but my own father, not so much.

"Mason!" he calls after me. His voice turns to white noise as the blood rushing in my ears gets louder and louder, drowning out all the bullshit.

The second I open the office door; he shuts the fuck up. He'll never let anyone hear us fighting. *Never.* Secrets are always left in the office. It's a family rule.

The door shuts with a loud thud and as I walk down the empty hall, the thin carpeting mutes the sound of my black leather oxfords smacking against the ground at an incessant pace.

Miss Geist looks up from her spot at her desk. Her eyes wrinkle as she tilts her head and gives me that smile that she always has for me. It's one that says, oh what have you done now?

Through the years, even after my mother's death, Miss Theresa Geist has given me that look. She's the only one who that showed any genuine regret when I had to deal with my mother's passing.

Weak, pathetic. You never let them see. That's all I got from my father and grandfather. Everyone else is dead and gone.

She clutches the small pendant on her thin silver necklace and her reprimanding smile changes to something more reserved when I look back at her. It's instantaneous and makes me halt in my steps. I know I must look pissed. And I am beyond furious. It's been two days since my father told me what he'd done all those months ago. It makes me fucking sick. Of course I knew what he'd done back then, deep down. I knew, but he never admitted it. He didn't have to though.

"He's being a prick," I mutter beneath my breath, waiting for the old lady to be a little bit more at ease. She doesn't know a damn thing that goes on behind these walls, and I don't owe her an explanation, but I can't help myself.

"Now, now," she says with a bit of playfulness although she's still shaken. She's not used to seeing me like this.

I give her a soft smile and wink, putting on the act I use so well. Maybe I have a soft spot for her, but I know who she works for and money is everything in this city.

"Have a good night, Mr. Thatcher," she tells me as she shuffles the papers on the desk, seeming somewhat less disturbed.

It's enough that it settles me and I push the double doors open with both hands and keep moving. The sound of my shoes slapping on the granite and the open air of the lobby filled with chatter soothes me.

But only for a moment.

It's not until I leave the building that my true feelings surface. The mask fades, and the fear sets in. I didn't know what my father was capable of.

I had an inkling, but I thought I'd always imagined it. I'd thought my memories weren't quite right. It's not that I expected more from him. I just fucking hate that I was right.

What's done is done and I can't stop what's been set in motion.

CHAPTER 2

Julia

Don't leave me alone, I cried and I screamed.
Don't leave me alone, my whole life demeaned.
You left me unguarded. My heart raw and bleeding.
You left me forever. The pain there left seething.
You left me here weak. Just a stone in the ground.
You left a place beside me, my pathetic life unbound.

BLOOD RED LIPS. It's called Black Honey, my favorite color. I've worn it since my freshman year of college and although I've dabbled in other colors at times, it's always been a staple in my beauty bag. I rub my lips together and smack them once as I look at myself in the mirror.

My skin's looking flawless with the Dior Airflash makeup and just a hint of blush I'm wearing. My lashes are thick and long. It's a timeless look, classic and clean. And it hides everything. My reddened skin and the dark circles under my eyes are nowhere to be found.

I don't look like the person I've become. This woman in the reflection, she's who I used to be. A very large part of me wants *this* woman back. I want to smile like I used to and hear the sound of a genuine laugh from my own lips.

My heart pangs at the thought though.

He'll never laugh again. It's as if any small moment of time that passes where he's forgotten for even a second is a disgrace. My eyes fall and I slip the cap back onto the tube of lipstick, tossing it into the pouch on my vanity.

No matter what I do, every little thing reminds me of *him.*

Trivial things, like the color of the granite he insisted we purchase for the remodel. The knobs on the bathroom drawers he hated and never failed to mention. Or the change he left in the cup holder in the Bentley. The small pile of dimes and pennies that clink together when I drive over speed bumps or a pothole. The same coins I refuse to touch. He put them there, and I can't bring myself to move them.

So stupid. Fucking pieces of copper renders me useless.

It may seem pathetic, but not to me. From my perspective, I'm being as strong as I can. I face the New York City judgement every day, putting my smile on and taking care of my life the best I'm able.

All the while I shove everything I'm feeling deep down inside. That's healthy, right?

I won't let them see me crumble. They want to. Oh, do they want me to. I can practically hear them licking their lips.

It was all over the papers when it happened.

Julia Summers, born into wealth and raised on the Upper East Side. She always did everything by the book and married young to her high school sweetheart, Jace Anderson. With a loving family, a handsome and doting husband and the social life every young woman in Manhattan dreams of, Jules had a perfect life. Until her husband suddenly passed away at the young age of twenty-eight, leaving the twenty-seven-year-old woman widowed and alone for the first time in her life.

Twenty-eight now.

They're waiting to see what I'll do next. Pens to the papers and cameras ready. There's nothing better for the gossipmongers.

They'd love to see me fall and I have, but not in front of their eyes. I'll keep my hair pinned up and my makeup flawless.

I know what they say though. They don't need to see the truth to figure it out themselves. There are whispers of alcohol. I don't have enough money for discretion; all my employees have sold out to the papers for a hint of what goes on behind these walls. When you live on the Upper East Side, every single person who struts in front of my home is looking for a crack in my veneer.

What's ironic is that there's no glamour here. Nothing noteworthy in the least. Just a woman who cries herself to sleep still. A woman who's struggling to move on. I suppose it's what I get though. I loved the cameras and lived for that spot in the gossip sections. This is what I deserve.

Days turn to weeks and weeks to months. Now that my husband's been gone for nearly eight months, I have plenty of cracks in this so-called perfect life. I'm fucking shattered.

I look back at myself and think, *I won't let them know it*, as I tug my dress down just slightly and smooth out the black lace.

I clear my throat as I turn off the light, snatching my phone and checking the text again.

Are you sure you don't need me to pick you up?

Kat's a sweetheart. She's always looking out for me. Of all my friends, she's the one who still texts me religiously, which is insane because she's constantly working and I have no idea how she finds the time.

My fingers *tap tap tap* away an answer. *No thank you. Leaving now.*

The Penrose is only twenty minutes away if there's no traffic.

Seeing how it's 9 p.m. on a Friday night, I'm prepared to sit in the back of the taxi for half the night.

A light sigh slips past my lips as I bend down to pick up my Louis Vuitton heels. They have a row of spikes up the back and a hot pink underside. They have exactly the touch of color and attitude I would've worn back then. I almost second guess the simple black dress I've picked out. It's a nod to Audrey Hepburn. But looking over my shoulder in the darkened bathroom mirror, all I see is an option for the funeral.

But I would've worn this back then. Back when I was happy and everything was how it was supposed to be. And don't I want to be that girl again?

I grit my teeth, holding the heels in one hand and the iron banister in the other as I descend the winding staircase.

I'm not *that* woman any longer, I've changed. I accept that, but I don't fucking like who I am now. Eight months of a pity party and being stuck in a rut is quite long enough, thank you. I'd like to say that Jace wouldn't want to see me like this... but I don't even know what Jace would want for me. I've quit wearing my ring, although it still sits on his nightstand. I'm ready to move on. I'm ready to find out who I really am.

Before I open the door, I glimpse out the large stained glass window in the foyer. It's all grey outside, and the hustle and bustle below is only a fraction of what it could be.

A faint patter of rain greets me when I step outside. I don't bother with an umbrella, simply tossing a trench coat on and quickly taking the steps to the street out front and hailing a cab. My heels click as I quickly wrap the belt tightly around me and tie my coat.

I could have called for someone to do this, to order me a cab so it would be waiting. I could ask for help with so many things. I'd rather do it myself though.

The breeze and rain feel *real*. The rain is cold to the touch and

I'm sure I'll be regretting it soon. But it's something different. And I don't want anyone's help. I just need time.

A cab pulls up within seconds and I lower my arm. Climbing in and shaking off the gathered rain from my jacket, the inside of the cab is warm and welcoming. I push the hair out of my face and say, "Penrose, please."

"You got it," the cabby says as he looks over his shoulder to look at me. His thinning black hair is oiled over and he's more than a little overweight. The buttons on his striped shirt are straining to keep it shut.

I can see the questions in his eyes, but just as he opens his mouth to ask *something*, I don't give a fuck what, I turn to look out of the closed window.

Everything outside is wet and dreary. The people walk quickly and a couple only about ten feet away are fighting over an umbrella. It's a cute little fight though and the tall man in a navy blue Henley lets the woman win. She's dressed for business, while he's in casual attire. But as soon as she takes full control of the umbrella, she walks closer to him and he wraps his arm around her waist.

I rip my eyes away and pick at my nails. It's little things like that I find unbearable. I bite the inside of my cheek and hold down the bitterness.

Luckily, the driver gets the picture. I'm not in the mood to talk, and the cab moves ahead, taking me away from my sanctuary and toward another test.

That's what these things really are. Tests.

It's only in this moment that I realize I'm really doing it. I've put it off so many times. I've given so many damn excuses for not meeting up with the girls.

Why today? I don't know. My heart sinks thinking that maybe I'm really getting over his death.

As much as I want to be the woman I used to be, happy and carefree, I don't want to forget him.

I lay my head back on the headrest and close my eyes, my Jimmy Choo clutch in my lap. Jace gave it to me last Christmas. I snort at the thought, running my fingers over the smooth hot pink leather. Really, I picked it out and he paid for it.

I close my eyes and take in a deep breath. It's calming, so damn calming driving in a quiet cab at night in the city. The quiet rumble of the engine and the white noise of the rain are a serene mix.

The last day I saw my husband was when we were watching my nephew Everett, so my sister could have a mother-daughter day with Lexi.

The thought of my nephew brings a smile to my face. With sandy blond hair that just barely covers his big blue eyes and a wide smile, you can't help but smile back at him. He was only a few months old back then. A brand new life in this world. That's the way it works, isn't it? Life and death going hand in hand.

I look forward, my eyes popping open and I stare out of the windshield when we stop far away from Second Avenue where the bar is located; it's just a bit of traffic is holding us up.

The cabby shrugs as he says, "We should be out of it soon." He's tense at the wheel, probably expecting me to snap at him, maybe blame him for taking the wrong route. More guilt washes down on me. I hate spreading negativity. I don't want other people to see me and judge me, or feel as though *this* is their fault. I'm not an ice bitch... or at least I don't mean to be.

I give him a soft smile, pulling my dress down slightly and placing my clutch in the middle seat, "I figured we'd run into something," I say easily. My voice comes out even and calm. It's the voice I use with my family. The kind of tone that says, *I'm okay, just tired.*

The cabby shifts, making the leather seat grumble and he tries to make small chat.

I nod my head and answer politely, but keep everything short and to the point. I can be accommodating to others and I want to be. I'm tired of being alone and pushing others away. It's just harder than I thought it would be.

After a moment of quiet, I look out of the window again. The rain's nearly stopped, and instantly the sidewalks are crowded as a result. The people were always there, just waiting under the awnings for protection. Not many people like to venture into the harsher nights with weather that washes away your makeup, and ruins even the best put-together look.

But they were waiting and ready to keep moving just the same. All they needed was a small break before they'd set out again. The only question is if there will be an awning to save them when the brutal downpour comes back.

The cabby stops and my eyes whip up to the sign on my right, my heart beating faster as I watch dozens of people walking in front of me on the sidewalk. Each going wherever it is that life has taken them. I don't know if I'm ready, but I'm here. My time is up and they're tired of waiting.

"Miss?" the cabbie asks. I shake my head slightly with quick motions and play off my hesitation, paying him and leaving a big tip as well. He deserves it for having to suffer my company.

"Have a good night," I tell him as I slip out, my heels hitting the slick asphalt and the door shutting behind me with a deafening click.

CHAPTER 3

Mason

The wind is harsh and brutal,
It makes you want to run.
The rain will cleanse your poor soul,
As it makes you come undone.
You can seek shelter from the damage
But its refuge is not your friend.
You knew from the beginning.
You knew how this would end.

IT FIGURES it would stop fucking raining the second I get in here. The bar is jam-packed as it always is, and the sounds of people chatting and glasses clinking welcome me. I can get lost in the crowds of people. I know they see me, but they don't *know* me.

This bar in particular is one of my favorites. It's always full. It's tufted leather seats are constantly filled, and the warm rich tones of the wooden ceiling and brick walls make it feel like home somehow.

My suit looks like every other fucker's suit. Well most of them. I run my fingers through my hair and shake off the rain as I shrug off my Armani jacket and toss it over the bar top at the very end.

It's been a long fucking day, and the last thing I need is go home alone. As soon as I lift my eyes lift, the bartender on me. Patricia's her name I think. She's in here every weekend.

"Whiskey?" she asks me. She never stops moving, shoveling ice into short glasses and pouring liquor like a pro. Unlike the other women in here, she's not looking for a man with deep pockets. She doesn't do chitchat either, which is one reason why I like sitting in this section. The other reason is that it's out of the way where I can just blend in and watch.

"Double," I answer her with a nod and slip out my cell phone out from my jacket pocket. I've only been gone for two hours, but I've got a dozen emails waiting for my attention. A huff of a grunt leaves me as another text from Liam pops up.

You coming out tonight?

Already out, I answer him as the glass hits the polished bar top and Patricia slides it over to me.

My phone pings as I lift the glass to my lips and let the cool liquor burn all the way down and warm my chest.

Where at?

I contemplate telling him. I like Liam. A lot. If I had any friends, he'd be one of them. But I don't trust anyone and after talking to my father today, I don't want to be around a damn soul.

A sarcastic laugh makes me grin as I realize I've come to a crowded bar to be alone. It's the truth though. In this city, you're always surrounded; there's never a place to hide unless it's in plain sight.

I down the rest of the liquor and tap the heavy glass against the bar top as I consider what to tell him. And that's when I hear it. Almost as if daring me to stay alone any longer. It's the gentle sound of a feminine laugh. It's genuine and it rings clear in the bar even though it's soft.

It's a soothing sound, a calming force in the chaos that surrounds us. As if everything is moving around me but the woman who uttered that sweet sound.

The smooth glass stays still as I look down the bar in search of her.

The rest of the crowd doesn't seem to notice, they continue with whatever the fuck they're saying and doing, but my eyes are drawn to my left. Through the throng of people, I just barely get a glimpse of her.

Blonde hair that's pulled back, showing off her pale skin covered in black lace.

A man at the very end leans away from the bar, digging into his back pocket for his wallet and giving me a clear view of her.

Those lips attract my gaze first. She licks her bottom lip before picking up a large glass of deep red wine. The color, from this distance at least, matches her lips perfectly. She smiles at something someone must have said and her shoulders shake, making the dark liquid swirl in her glass and bringing a blush to her high cheek bones.

She tosses her hair to the side, it's damp from the rain and her fingers tease the ends as she brings her tendrils over her shoulder, wrapping them around her finger while she sips her wine.

It's when she looks away from whoever she's been giving her attention to that my heart stops and my curiosity is piqued.

Without their eyes on her, her expression morphs into something else. I finally see her eyes, the lightest of blues with flecks of silver speckled throughout, and that's when I really see her. Not just the image of what she's portraying.

Pain is clear as day.

It's the lie though, how fucking good she was at hiding it, that's what really gets me. Even I was fooled.

People can hide behind a smile or a laugh, every fucker in here can pretend to be something and someone they're not.

The truth is always there though and I'm damn good at recognizing it. Your eyes can never hide two things: age and emotion. Hers speak to me in a way nothing else can.

But had I never looked just then when she thought no one was watching, she never would have shown me willingly.

She straightens her shoulders and I see her profile, her expression and the corners of my lips turn down. Not only do I know her pain; I know her name. I know everything about her.

Julia Summers.

My blood chills as she turns back to the table and the smile slips back into place on her face just as the man at the end of the bar takes a step forward, obscuring her from my vision. As if the moment of clarity and recognition was just for me in that moment. Like fate wanted me to know how close I was to her.

I keep my eyes on the bar, doing my best to listen, but her voice is silent or lost in the mix of chatter throughout the crowded place.

"Another?" Patricia's voice sounds close, closer than she usually is. I lift my head to see her standing right in front of me, both hands on the bar and waiting.

I nod my head with my brows pinched, shaking off the mix of emotions. This city is a small place with worlds always colliding, but I've never seen her in person. Only in a photograph. Only that once. I'm sure it's her though. I've never been this sure of anything.

The ice clinks in the glass and I watch as the liquid slips over each cube, cracking them and filling the crevices.

"You okay?" Patricia asks me. It's odd. In the year or so since I've been coming here, she's never bothered to make small talk. It's why I don't mind her.

I give her a tight smile as I reply, "I'm fine." I reach her eyes and widen my smile, relaxing my posture and leaning back slightly.

She eyes me warily as she mutters, "You don't look fine."

It takes me a moment before I shrug it off and say, "I'm alright, just tired."

She nods once and goes back to minding her own business, sliding me the whiskey and moving back to the other customers.

I tap my pointer finger against the glass, looking casually down the bar.

She's hidden from view, but I know she's there.

CHAPTER 4

Julia

Carry on for that is life.
You have no choice; you have no right.
Just be still, for that is death.
Do not dare move, you have no breath.
What shame to stay, where life is void.
What could be beauty, is destroyed.
The past is gone and so shall be you,
So long before your life is through.

MY BODY TINGLES with another sip of cabernet.

It's my third glass and it's only tasting sweeter on my lips. The tips of my fingers always feel it first. That familiar buzz that makes my body feel a bit heavy and my mind light.

"I can't believe your license plate says *Alimony*," Maddie says into her wine glass as she snickers again. She's laughing so hard, the white zinfandel splashes onto her lips, but she doesn't care. She merely smiles and takes a deep gulp.

Suzette answers with a shrug and a cocky smirk, "Fucker had it coming to him." Her bright pink lipstick smudges against her glass of Long Island Ice Tea and she wipes it away with her napkin as Maddie continues to laugh. Sue's given herself a makeover since her divorce is finalized. Currently she's sporting jet black hair with a blunt bob cut and bangs to go with her snippy attitude.

"Did you really have to put it on display like that though?" Maddie asks still smiling from ear to ear and tossing her drink back.

Maddie's young and naive and thinks Prince Charming is out there, so you should always be ready. Sue has a marriage, a divorce, and fifteen years on Maddie, so that fuck you side-eye doesn't go unnoticed, at least not by me.

I love her dearly, but Maddie's horrible at picking up on Suzette's feelings, but it's plain as day to me, even as tipsy as I am, that Sue doesn't want to talk about it. Her license plate is just one more way for Sue to make fun of her divorce before anyone else can. That asshole put her through hell and she came out cold as ice to all men. Well except the ones she likes to sink her claws into after a few Long Islands.

Sue leans back in the white leather booth, keeping the glass in her hand and shrugs again as she says, "What says 'Fuck you, mother fucker' like a red Ferrari with *that* license plate?"

Kat pipes up from her corner of the booth, rolling her eyes and taking a sip of her Pepsi, "I think it says, 'Don't touch this bitch' to every man in the city."

A sly smile slips onto Sue's face. "Thank fuck," she says as she sets her drink down and stretches her arms over her head. "Maybe all these bastards will finally leave me alone then." The other girls laugh and I join in although my heart's not in it. My nerves are shot just being out here tonight. Sue's directly across from me, and both of us are seated at the ends of the semi-circular booth. Kat to my right, then Maddie.

Sue's just going through her own personal tragedy. In a way you could call it a death, not like mine, but not unlike it either. I know all this is just a defense mechanism; I wish the other girls could see it too.

"Another round?" The waiter startles me and I nearly spill my glass as I gasp and back away. All the eyes within the vicinity turn to me, everyone within the vicinity and I do what I do best, I let out a small laugh and play it off. Maybe I'm even more like Sue than I realized.

"Sorry," I say a bit too loud, playing up how tipsy I am, but sweetly and gently placing my hand on the waiter's arm. His crisp white shirt is soft under my fingers as I lean in and say, "I'm so sorry, I hope I didn't spill any on you."

That's all it takes for everyone to go about their own business, but my heart's still beating wildly. Some eyes linger. I'm aware they recognize me. My eyes stop across the room; frozen by a gaze I know all too well.

They belong to a woman in her late sixties, Margo Pierce. She's an heiress and an influential investor in the city. Her large sapphire cocktail rings appear even more over the top as she holds a simple glass of champagne with both hands. For a woman in her sixties, she wears her age well. From her perky breasts to the delicate skin around her eyes, not an inch of her hasn't been through some procedure or another. It's all done in good taste though.

The last time I saw her was at a casino, the night I got the phone call. I can still remember the sounds of the machines and the bright colorful lights. A glass of rosé in my right hand as I sat perched on a bar stool in the center of the casino. At the Mohegan, the bar is elevated. I could see so many other guests playing slots and sitting at the card tables; it was packed that night.

Just like tonight, I was with the girls and we were enjoying ourselves and the atmosphere. We were taking a break from roulette with cocktails and Sue was cursing out her husband when the phone rang. I only picked it up because it was odd for my mother to call me so late.

Kat leaned in to order from the bartender as I placed the phone to my ear, turning a bit to my left for a hint of privacy. I didn't show them anything, keeping a pleasant smile on my face as I answered.

When I heard my mother's voice on the other end, the smile vanished and the sounds turned to dead air.

I could barely make out my mother's voice, just a few words here and there, but I knew something was wrong. Very wrong.

My heart raced, and the shock caused my body temperature to drop so low that I was shivering.

He's dead. I heard her words clear as day as I got to the entrance of the casino. My heels clipped the large rug that covered the granite floor at the entrance. I stumbled forward, my short dress riding up and my left heel nearly falling off. My knees hit the hard ground and the phone fell from my hand.

Jace is dead. That's what she said. *Jace, my Jace, is dead*, I thought.

I imagine they thought I was drunk. I would have assumed that if I'd seen someone fall the way I had.

Margo Pierce was there to help me. Those damn cocktail rings were digging into my arm as she helped lift me up. I stood there on wobbly legs just trying to breathe, but when I looked up and into her eyes, I could tell she knew.

I knew in that moment it was real. I could lie to myself, or I could have hung up and driven home, all the while in denial. But the sympathy in her eyes was damning.

I rip my eyes away from hers and return back to the girls, to tonight, leaving that night in the past, right where it belongs. I ignore the way my hand itches to drain the glass of wine and order another and push my hair back over my shoulders, trying to relax. Trying to shake off the unwanted memories.

"I think you're flagged," Kat mutters into her glass even as her eyes meet mine. Her sandy brunette hair is colored with a subtle ombre and she's worn her eyeliner in a cat-eye fashion. I don't know why, but I can't stop looking at it. Like if I can just concentrate on her makeup, everything else will go the fuck away.

"No such thing," Sue's quick to come to my defense, a smile on her face. "Drink up, girly." She gives me a wink and it forces a smile to my face. It didn't take long for the girls to come find me that night, crying alone in the back of the limo.

I blink a few times to keep the tears away. It was months and months ago, but sometimes the pain comes back full force. I don't know that it will ever go away and if it does, surely that would be a tragedy. I don't know where the grief and mourning ends and my life begins again, but I'd like to find it.

I push the nearly empty glass away, watching the dark liquid pool into the very bottom and sigh deeply. I can't seem to force the smile to stay on my face. The once easy mask isn't slipping into place. Progress is all I need though. I remind myself of my motto: Seek for progress, not perfection.

"Let's talk about something and someone else," I suggest.

My skin pricks at the back of my neck as I feel a set of eyes on me. The anxiety comes back and I put on my best fake smile, staring straight ahead as Maddie starts listing off what's wrong with her last rendezvous.

I don't know who it is, but someone's watching me. It could be the papers, but every time I've gone out, they've approached me before I've even noticed them. I debate on taking a casual look over my shoulder. I thought I felt someone watching me earlier, but maybe I was wrong.

It's all in your head, I tell myself again.

"You know enough time has passed," I hear Sue say from across the table. I look up at her dark eyes twinkling with mischievousness.

"Enough time for what?" Maddie asks Sue. Maddie's the quintessential younger sister of our group and I swear most of Sue's references go right over her head.

Sue motions toward me, and it's only then that I take in her words. I clear my throat and look away, feeling a blush rise to my cheeks. "When I said someone else…" I mutter playfully and pick up the glass, tilting it all the way up in the air and throwing my head back to get the last few drops.

The girls laugh it off, but there's a certain gravity in Sue's eyes.

She lowers her voice and looks at me in the eyes as she says, "We just want you to be happy."

"It's 'we' now?" I ask her suddenly feeling defensive. They've been talking about me behind my back?

Sue shrugs and Kat's quick to put a hand on top of mine. She twists in her spot and the white leather booth squeaks under her skinny ass. "We were just talking earlier." My brow rises as she takes in a breath and tries to find the right words.

"We want you happy again," Maddie says from her seat next to Kat. Her hands make two sharp motions emphasizing "happy again" as she leans back in her seat and looks straight ahead, avoiding my eyes on her.

Of course they'd talk about me. I'm not shocked by that at all. I can't explain why it feels like a betrayal though. Why my throat seems to go dry and then itch as if I'm going to cry. Why wouldn't they? Everyone else is.

"Hey, Jules," Kat's voice is soft, placating even.

I pull my hand away from her and suck in a breath, "it's fine," I whisper, grabbing my clutch.

"Don't go," Sue's quick to sit forward and plead. "It wasn't-"

"Just to the powder room," I blurt out. "I just need to freshen up," I tell them with a tight smile, standing up and pulling down my dress.

"Do you want company?" Kat asks, already sliding out behind me.

"I just need a minute," I say and shake my head, and give her pleading eyes.

I can handle this, and I'm more than ready to. I just need *something*. A breath of fresh air maybe. Or a drink of water or something stronger. I don't know what, but I know I need a damn minute to figure it out.

CHAPTER 5

Mason

Just when you least expect it,
The sins come back to play.
They tempt you and lure you,
To go back to yesterday.
Before you knew what waited here,
Before you knew the lies.
Before, you had a choice to save her,
Before your own demise.
But before is already gone,
It's in the past where it will stay
So look forward, not backward,
For all you have is today.

THE ANXIOUS FEELING deep in my gut won't quit. It only gets more intense as Julia walks behind me, politely maneuvering her small frame between the crowd of people. I watch her from my periphery, listening to the rhythmic sound of her heels and watching how her hips sway gently.

She doesn't notice me, which is by my design, but still it aggravates me. She passes so close behind me on her way to the restrooms that I catch a hint of her sweet scent. No doubt it's perfume, a gentle floral with a citrus of some sort, but as it fills my lungs I can't help but grip the bar top tighter to keep myself from following her.

Ever since I caught a glimpse of her, I haven't been able to move or get her out of my head. For months, I haven't thought twice about her. Each time her picture swept into my thoughts, I pushed it away.

But she's here now, so close that I could touch her.

I can't approach her though. How fucked up would that be?

Her eyes haunt me, but her body tempts me. And she doesn't know a damn bit of the truth. I can't cross that line. That's not the man I want to be. Not anymore.

I down the whiskey and slide the empty glass forward.

As I stand up abruptly, the stool slides backward and bumps into someone. I turn to look over my shoulder while reaching into my back pocket for my wallet. "Sorry," I say without thinking and then stare at Julia.

Her eyes still aren't on me as she waves off my apology, looking at the bottles lining the back of the bar before finally setting her gorgeous blue eyes on me.

She shakes her head just slightly, making her hair fall off her shoulder and exposing more of her bare skin. "It's fine," she says sweetly and then walks forward, stepping up to the bar on my right, coming closer to me. Like a lamb stepping into the lion's den, teasing and taunting unknowingly.

She's so fucking close to me, so damn alluring. The black dress clings to her curves. Her hips are wide and I can just imagine how they'd feel to hold as I took her from behind. I can feel Patricia's eyes flicker to me as Julia orders, but I can't help staring at Julia.

I swallow thickly, leaning my forearms against the bar and trying to act casual, getting that much closer to her.

She doesn't know anything and she doesn't have to. She'll never know the truth and this is my chance to learn more about who the pretty face in the picture is.

"Julia, right?" I ask her. My heart pounds as, thinking why the hell would I admit that I know anything at all about her. I don't intend to lie to her though. Nothing but lies of omission. I've heard her name in the social circles. Her family is well known so I doubt she'll be surprised that I recognize her.

"Jules," she says warmly, now looking at me differently than she did a moment ago. She seems to do a double take and a hint of playfulness sparkles in her eyes. It's as if I'm suddenly what she's been looking for. Or maybe *who* she's been waiting for.

"Ah, Jules." I tap my fingers on the bar and look away for a moment. What the fuck am I doing? This isn't just playing with fire, this is worse. It's asking to be burned and shoving my fists into the coals.

Patricia sets two shots of what look like chilled tequila in front of Jules. I eye them and then her as she throws the first one back without thinking twice. Her slender fingers slip around the second one, ready to down it as well.

I can fucking feel the pain coming off her in waves. She's drowning it in alcohol. She's good at hiding her emotions on the surface, but her actions speak so much louder than words.

"Not gonna share?" I ask her teasingly, more to keep her from drinking it then the desire to have it for myself.

She licks her lips and smiles. "You want it?"

Goddamn, does she know how she's coming off right now? She's already testing me, because just hearing those words slip between her lips has my dick straining in my pants. Yes, I fucking want it. She's practically forbidden. The only woman in this city I should be ashamed to look in the eyes.

"If you're offering," I answer her with a flirtatiousness I don't recognize. She blushes and tucks her hair back behind her ear. As she pulls her eyes away from me, she catches a glimpse of something across the room that rips the happiness from her in an instant.

I throw the shot back but keep my eyes on her. The cold liquid burns. I was right about it being tequila. It's strong too. Stronger than I expected and it takes the breath from me, making my chest feel tight, but then it relaxes me all the way down.

I hold up two fingers for Patricia, "Another two," I order and slip the stool I'd been sitting on over to Jules as I continue to stand. "Let me get you another," I offer her. Instantly her eyes come back to me.

I watch as they swirl with a mix of questions. The vulnerability is clearly there and that only makes her that much more enticing.

"I'm not sure I should," she says softly. Her honesty is so raw, so genuine.

"You really shouldn't," I answer her with complete honesty as well. She deserves that much. She's little Red Riding Hood in fuck-me-heels and I'm worse than the Big Bad Wolf. I lean forward, knowing I'm breaking every rule I have and bring my lips just inches from her ear.

Her fingers tighten on the edge of the stool as I whisper, "But you want to. And this is so much better than whatever you were going to do." I'm not sure if my confession is for her or for me, but either way, I've convinced myself.

My rough voice and hot breath make goosebumps rail down her shoulder. Her nipples pebble under her dress and I can just barely make them out as I pull away from her, offering her space and an out.

She could leave if she wanted to. She could walk away. Fuck, she could call me an asshole if she wanted to, and I'd sit here and do my best to pretend I'll never go after her again. In this moment, I can't say with confidence I'd never approach her again.

It takes a moment for Jules to pull herself together. She stands there in what seems like a daze. It's only when Patricia sets the shot glasses down, spilling just a touch of the chilled tequila over the edge of one glass, that she comes back to me.

I take the one closest to her and hold it out to her. She keeps her eyes on me but accepts it.

"Here's to things we know we shouldn't do," I tell her with a smile, lifting my glass and extending it for a toast.

Slowly, so very slowly, that bit of happiness comes back to her. Her eyes keep flickering with uncertainty to the floor and across the room.

"Here's to happiness," she says with feigned confidence, making her shoulders straighter as she clinks her glass against mine and then throws it back. She slams hers down on the bar while I'm still left holding mine and watching her every move.

I toss it back as she picks up her clutch, obviously ready to pay for the shots.

"Don't," I tell her with more strength in my voice than I should have used. I lighten my tone as I say, "It's on me." I hesitate then add, "I was just getting ready to leave."

She watches me warily, but I look toward Patricia as I get out my own wallet. All the while paying attention to Jules in my periphery.

"Well, thank you... what's your name?" she asks.

"Mason," I answer her hoping she's never heard of me, but she brightens and nods her head.

"Thatcher. Yes, I thought I recognized you." She bites the inside of her cheek as something hits her. Her expression falls slightly. "I'm sorry to hear-"

I cut off her apology, and then pass my card to Patricia. "To happiness, right?" It hurts me to say the words, but I don't bother to hide it.

That only makes her lips turn down into an alluring frown, somehow making her look even more beautiful. We're both in pain. Both getting over something. Only this shit I did to myself and she's collateral damage.

She catches the glimpse of someone behind me and it makes her turn to the bar again, her back straight and the playfulness gone.

"To happiness, and to the things that we want," I tell her as I sign the receipt and leave the pen on the bar. I spear my fingers through my hair, feeling the heat of the moment and the buzz of the liquor starting to affect me.

I glance at her and watch as she closes her eyes. It's affecting her too. She's easy prey -- beautiful, naive, innocent. I'm an asshole for doing it, but I can't help that I want her.

"I'm gonna get out of here," I say then let my eyes roam down her body, not hiding what I want from her. "You wanna come with?"

CHAPTER 6

Julia

It's in pain that choices are clear.
We show ourselves what we desire.
We may fight it, want to deny it,
but in weakness, we fall in the fire.

To the things that we want.

Mason's words keep echoing in my ears. I know I'm buzzed, but the odd mix of anxiety and relaxation running through me are from something else. It's the realization that I'm at a crossroads. I'm standing in front of an open door and I know that going through would change everything. It would put my world into motion again, moving me forward, shoving me from the stagnant still place I've been in these last few months.

There would be no way to go back, but there's no telling who I'd be once I'm on the other side. My body is ringing with desire and adrenaline.

Mason Thatcher. I've heard of him. The pictures I've seen don't do his broad shoulders and muscular frame justice. The rough stubble on his jaw begs me to reach up and brush my fingertips against it. He's tall and handsome... and a player. A man I shouldn't be caught dead talking to. My husband would have killed me for having drinks with a man like Mason.

But Jace has left me all alone. And Mason's so much more than I thought I could want in a man.

My body temperature rises as the tequila drifts into my blood. I lick my lower lip and then rip my eyes from his hard body. I noticed his hands first, rough and callused although he's in a suit. It's clear they're from years of hard work, something most of the men in here know little about. Actual manual labor.

I try to relax some and casually lean against the bar, slipping my pointer finger into the empty shot glass and forcing it onto its side. I don't know why and it probably makes me appear drunker than I am, but I don't care.

"Mason, do you like tequila?" I ask him and this time when I speak, there's a bit of flirtiness in my voice. Guilt weighs heavily in my chest, but only briefly before the alcohol numbs the memories. I've been alone for too long.

Mason's steel grey eyes roam over the curves of my waist and ass. He's bold, licking his lips and then taking a step forward to lean against the bar with me. He's close enough that the heat of his body makes me that much hotter.

I want to know what it's like for a man like him to pin me beneath him. To take me how he wants me. I close my eyes as the heat rises into my cheeks from the intensity of his stare.

"I do," he replies and his voice is low and rough, and it does bad things to me. I rest my head in my hand, loving and hating the way the alcohol soothes the pain.

I'm ready to move on, aren't I? Maybe not, but I'm ready to *feel*. I look back at him, realizing he's just answering my question.

I'm a bit more than tipsy, but I'm still here and present and I know what I want.

Even if I'll hate myself in the morning, it's one night of not going back to that large, empty house alone.

The tight pull of two small hands at my waist and Sue's loud voice, make my heart scream in my chest and I swear to God I almost have a damn heart attack. I feel like a child caught with her hand in the cookie jar.

"Jules, Jasper's out front," Sue starts talking to me like she has no idea she just scared the shit out of me.

My heart pounds in my chest as I turn to face her fully, my eyes flickering from the man candy on my right and then back to her.

Caught red handed.

It takes a moment for me to realize what Sue said and a moment for her to catch on to what I was about to do.

She eyes Mason cautiously, but before she can say a word, I speak up, "Jasper?"

Although it comes out like a question, it's more of a curse.

Sue gives me a sympathetic look as she explains, "The exhibition at Ruppert Park must've ended." Jasper's with the New York Post. And every fucking time he sees me, he has a question and I know whatever I say will end up quoted in the papers the very next morning. He's not kind like the others. I would rather not see Jasper's scrawny ass right now.

I let out a heavy breath, looking through the crowd and towards the entrance. I don't feel like dealing with this shit.

"And what are you doing here?" Sue's question is directed at Mason who's standing behind me, leaning against the bar and looking sexy as fuck. He doesn't seem to mind the interruption at all. He gives Sue a lazy smile that brings back the heat between my thighs full force.

"Just leaving actually." Jesus, his voice is as smooth as velvet.

One split second passes and a wide grin spreads across Sue's face, her dark hair sways, brushing against her cheek as she knowingly looks between the two of us. I lean backward, gripping the stool behind me and wanting an escape. It's one thing to flirt with the idea, it's another for everyone to know it.

Sue looks pointedly at Mason's cock and raises a brow, which only makes me want to bury my face in my hands.

"Are you ready to leave?" I ask Sue. I take a step away from Mason, gripping my clutch in my hand tighter and feeling completely ready to get the fuck out of here. There's not enough tequila in the world to numb the sobriety that the mention of Jasper brings me.

"You two get out of here," Sue says, stopping me in my tracks.

"What'd you say your name was?" she asks Mason.

"Mason Thatcher." He extends a hand to Sue and she takes his hand coyly with both of hers. I can't fucking help that I stare daggers at where their hands meet. This possessiveness I feel towards Mason is something I'm not used to, and I don't fucking like it. There's no reason I should even give a damn. He was just a fun idea. But mostly, a *bad* idea.

"Mason," Sue says and her voice drips with sex appeal. It always does. She's a cold-hearted bitch to some but just as vivacious and insatiable as she was ten years ago when I first met her during my freshman year of college.

She leans in slightly and I get a good look down her blouse. Her necklace shifts so that the thin gold chain and glittering emerald jewel rest on her perky breasts, but when I look up, Mason's only looking into her eyes. "You take good care of my girl tonight, Mason." Sue looks back at me and that roguish look in her eyes makes me smile.

"I plan on it," Mason answers and releases her hand.

"Just one minute," Sue holds up her pointer finger and grips my wrist, moving me an entire foot away from Mason and closer to the powder room as if he can't hear us. I keep myself from rolling my eyes.

I don't want her to judge me, or to hate me. I just want her to understand. Out of all the girls, I think she will. More than anything, I know I want to get out of here with a stranger. It makes me feel dirty and shameful, but right now it's what I want.

"It's nothing serious." The words come out in a defensive tone.

"It is for me," Sue says. My lungs stall at her words. She shifts her weight and looks over her shoulder towards our booth. I can't see either Kat or Maddie although I know they're still there. "You need this." Sue stares into my eyes, the look so serious I'm caught off guard.

"The question is," she lowers her voice and leans into me, "are we telling the others?" When she pulls away, gripping my elbows in her hands and raising her brow, I know everything's going to be okay.

I hesitate, looking back at Mason and then bite the inside of my cheek. "I don't want to lie to them," I answer honestly.

"Then you two go out the back. And do it fast before I go tell them and before Jasper can get his skinny, organic, vegan-eating ass inside."

I snicker at Sue's response, but the reality of what I'm doing is setting in. I lean forward as Sue lets go and I grip her hand before she can turn and leave me alone with my soon-to-be one-night stand.

"Tell me I'm not a bad person." The words slip out before I can even think about what I'm saying. I try to keep the smile on my face, but it wavers.

"Stop that shit right now." Sue's face is completely serious as she points her finger at me.

I nod my head, willing the emotions to go back down to being buried deep inside of me as if they don't deserve to surface in this moment.

"You are a beautiful, strong, kind woman," Sue tells me and I look her in the eyes although I don't share her conviction. "And there is not a goddamn thing wrong with getting laid."

The bit of humor helps me feel a sense of relief, but it's small. Her expression softens. "You just need a little something to kick start your happiness again."

To happiness.

"I do." I nod my head.

Sue's not one to get emotional. Not in the least and true to her nature she skirts around the way my voice cracks as she takes a half step closer to me. "Then get over there and let Mr. Yes-please-fuck-me-with-my-ankles-pinned-behind-my-head- "

A laugh escapes me before she can even finish and I wipe under my eyes as I shake my head. "Can you even put your legs behind your head?"

"For the right man, I can do a lot of shit." She looks back at Mason and then to me.

"Just have fun tonight," she says making light of the situation, but it's calming. I want to be like her. I want to believe it's completely harmless.

I nod my head as she turns from me, leaving me alone with Mason.

Alone to do bad things and make bad decisions. But at least I'm doing *something*.

It's then that I notice a few eyes watching. Including Margo, who's taking covert glances. My anxiety keeps ramping up, daring me to go through with it and that's when he wraps his hand around my hip and pulls me into him. Bringing my back to his front and whispering in my ear.

"You ready to go?" he asks me, his hot breath traveling down my sensitive skin and making my body feel alive.

I don't close my eyes; I just stare straight ahead. I don't care that they can see. The city can talk; I'll deny it all.

"Will you hold me afterward?" I whisper my one request before I realize what I've said.

His body stills behind me and I close my eyes, hating that I've ruined this before it's even started. It's a one-night stand, nothing more. No emotions.

"Until the morning?" he asks me. My heart beats again, in rhythm with his.

I nod my head, my hair rubbing against his hard chest and his thumb brushing against the black fabric of my dress.

Just until morning.

CHAPTER 7

What's wrong is tempting. What's forbidden is best.
It's the past that's waiting and putting you to the test.
If she can forgive, it would all be made right.
But she'd have to know, to forgive, and that won't happen tonight.

WILL YOU HOLD ME AFTERWARD?

I'm calm on the outside, as if there's not a damn thing wrong with what I'm doing. I don't know what's come over me

The Benz's alarm beeps as I unlock it and open Julia's door for her. Her heels are muted on the wet asphalt as she rounds me and slips easily into the luxurious leather seat. Her soft blue eyes look up at me as she tucks her hair behind her ear and then settles the clutch in her lap as she murmurs, "Thank you."

I merely smile and close her door, the keys jingling as I walk to the driver side, my heart beating wildly.

This is a fucking mistake. I don't hold women afterward. I don't fuck women who I should stay far away from.

But I'm also a selfish prick, and I'd be a liar if I said I didn't want her. And what I want, I get.

I clear my throat as I start the car, the purr of the engine and soft classical music filling the cabin.

As I look over my shoulder to back out of the parking space, Jules clears her throat, "Are we going to..." she starts to ask and then a beautiful blush colors her cheeks.

I can't help the smirk on my face at her shyness or the way my cock jumps in my pants. I put the car into drive and peek at her before leaving the tight parking lot and heading down Second Avenue. "Where are we headed, sweetheart?" My fingers itch to rest against her bare thigh as her dress rides up slightly. I place my hand on the shifter instead, stopping at a red light and looking over to her.

She squirms in her seat and I fucking love it. It's easy to forget with her. Maybe that's what it is. Maybe that's why I just can't say no and walk away. If I can convince her, then it'll all be alright. I'm her downfall and she's my savior.

"My place?" I ask her to put her out of her misery. She's quick to nod, glancing at me and then looks down to her hands in her lap.

I'm enjoying this way too much. I turn to look out of the driver's side window and ignore that voice in the back of my head that tells me I'm a Grade A prick for doing this to her.

"Thank you," she says softly, grabbing my attention once again as the light turns green and the traffic moves again.

"For heading out the back and away from all that..." she waves her hands in the air before falling back against the seat and concluding, "bullshit."

I nod my head once, looking back to the windshield and twisting my hand around the leather steering wheel.

"No problem," I say easily, but I can feel her need to talk, to tell me why and who and everything else that's on her mind and I'm not interested in hearing it. I wait for it, staring straight ahead, but nothing comes. Just silence as we drive to the sounds of Tchaikovsky.

It's only fifteen minutes to my place at this rate, but the time can't pass fast enough. Every second of silence is a second I consider turning back.

"Do you always do this?" Jules asks and breaks up the quiet.

"What's that?"

"This," she says sleepily, her cheek resting against the seat as she looks at me.

"Hmm?" I still don't understand her question.

"Pick up women-" she stops and rolls her eyes before she even finishes. I used to, without thinking twice. But that was before Avery. Before my father and all this hell I've been thrown into.

"So you do, do this often?" she asks me again and I have to hold back my smile at her brazen question.

"I'm not going to answer that, Jules." My voice comes out a little harder than I wanted and she shrinks back some.

It's tense for a moment and I flick on the turn signal as we turn down a deserted street. So, close. I can't lose her now. "I don't," I tell her simply.

She peeks over at me, and I can tell she doesn't believe me.

"I don't usually take a woman home." *And I sure as fuck don't do sleepovers.* I grind my teeth remembering how I said I would. How her innocent plea made me weak. "It's been a long time for me."

"Why your house then?" she asks with curiosity.

"Because I like to sleep in my own bed."

Her brows pinch for a moment, and then she struggles to hold back a laugh. It catches me off guard but then I remember how much she drank. I'm still feeling a bit of the tequila myself. My tolerance is high as fuck, so if I'm feeling it, she must be wasted. The realization drains the blood from my face.

"How are you feeling?" I ask her.

"Fine," she says and then covers her mouth with her hand.

"Are you drunk?" I ask her. She doesn't look like it in the least.

She purses her lips and shakes her head as she says, "Nope. Just right." She stretches in the seat, covering another yawn as I pull up to my gates.

I eye her for a moment and then brush it off.

I know Jules comes from money, born into this lifestyle like me, so I'm surprised to see the admiration on her face when we arrive. "Your home is beautiful." Her voice is even and sincere. I'm proud of my home. I built it myself. Liam helped design it for the engineering purposes, but it was all based on my ideas and plans.

I pull up in the driveway and Jules grips her clutch a bit tighter as her phone starts vibrating.

She doesn't pay attention as I roll up to the front of the house. She's too busy reading a text and by the look on her face and the way she shoves the phone back into her clutch, it's not good.

"Everything alright?" I ask more to make sure I'm getting her ass into my bed than anything else.

For a split second, only a moment, I think it's someone who knows what happened. Someone who saw what I did, although I don't think anyone could have possibly seen. My muscles coil and my knuckles turn white as I grip the shifter, putting the car into park and searching her face for answers.

She blows a bit of hair out of her face and looks anywhere but at me.

"It's fine," she answers me, but I know she's lying. And I don't fucking like it. Apparently, I'm a hypocrite as well as a prick.

"Tell me what's wrong." The command comes out easily as I grip her chin in my hand and force her to look at me.

Her eyes go wide and I almost second-guess it. *Almost*. But then she caves to me.

"My friends just found out."

I cock a brow at her, rubbing the rough pad of my thumb over her bottom lip. "Found out?" I ask her. She parts them slightly and judging by the way she leans into me; my touch is all she needs to loosen up.

"I don't do this... often or... ever-" I lean in and press my lips to hers, stopping her explanation. I move my hand to her cheek and then behind her head as she deepens the kiss. Her hot mouth opens and her tongue massages mine in swift, strong strokes.

I groan into her open mouth, our breath mingling as my dick hardens to fucking stone.

"Forget about them," I tell her as I break the kiss and pull away from her. She's left breathless, her eyes still closed as I open my door and start to get out, taking the keys with me.

I almost close the door and miss her whispering, "I'll forget about it all."

But I heard her. I heard the whisper, the raw vulnerability and truth in her statement.

I wish I hadn't.

CHAPTER 8

Julia

Just one touch. Just one time.
Just one kiss. Just one crime.
Take me far. Take the pain.
Take it all. Break the chain.
Leave me here. When you're done.
I'll survive. But you'll have won.

I'VE NEVER HAD a one-night stand before.

Not once.

It's not like I've ever had a thing against them and Lord knows my friends enjoy them, with or without discretion. I've just never... it's never happened. My body heats everywhere, one place a bit more than others.

My thoughts race as Mason wraps his hand around my waist

and leads me to the front door. The chill in the night air is sobering. I can't explain how anxiety is shooting through me. My breathing comes in a little faster now that the alcohol's all but worn off.

All I can think about is how even the pace of our footsteps are and how I've never done this before.

I'm doing it. I'm going to sleep with a stranger. *I'm going to sleep with someone other than Jace.*

Jace and I met as children, paired up in boarding school. I've never been with anyone else. I'm so sheltered, I always have been. I nearly have a panic attack at the thought and my shoe slips on the paved steps, nearly making me fall, but I catch myself.

Mason's quick to grab onto my elbow and waist; his hands are hot on my body. It's like a shock, as something violent inside of me reacts to his very touch. I instinctively pull away, only just then releasing a breath I didn't know I'd been holding.

Eight months alone... even longer since I've been touched. Moving on has never been such a dominating thought, or so terrifying.

I wrap my arms around my chest, fueled by both fear and desire. My pulse quickens as I look back over my shoulder and towards his car. Towards an escape.

Mason straightens his shoulders, squaring them and hitting the keys against his leg once. The jingle catches my attention. It's the only sound in the cold, dark night.

I stand frozen as I look into his eyes. I'm a fool for doing this. It's not me. Not the woman I am today and not the woman I was before I lost my husband. Mason's steel grey gaze searches my own and I feel lost all over again.

A wave of denial is running through me. He doesn't want me. Why would he? What was I thinking?

I part my lips ready to give an excuse, a lie, or even the truth. Anything to just go back in time and avoid this disaster.

To run just like I've been doing for the past eight months.

Didn't I say I needed a change? I said I needed something drastic, but that was back when the alcohol was strong and we were surrounded by a crowd of people.

Mason is tempting, gorgeous, and confident. But I can't handle a man like him. I can't deal with a situation like this.

Weak and alone. A low whisper from the self-loathing bitch inside of me resonates in my ears. I slam my lips shut tight without uttering a word, hating that she's right.

I won't leave. I suck in a breath and force myself to be determined. Right or wrong, I don't give a fuck.

A moment passes with the two of us just standing still in front of his porch. Only three, four-foot wide steps are between us and his deep navy front door. I just have to get there.

My eyes flicker from the door to Mason. My palms are growing sweaty and my blood heats as he takes a single step closer to me. It's only one step, but with it is something powerful. His height, his scent, and his very dominance overwhelms me when he's this close. He radiates desire and my mind may be having second thoughts, but my body is pulled to him, magnetized by his presence.

It's calming. Shockingly so, as I let my body move forward, closing the small space between us. He trails a finger down my collarbone, lightly, testing my reaction.

"I want to touch you Jules," he says softly, forcing my gaze back to his all-consuming stare. I hadn't imagined it'd be this intense. Not in the bar and not in his Mercedes. He didn't push, and he didn't do anything to make me feel trapped. How odd, now that we're out in the open with no locked doors and no enclosed in spaces, it's only now that I feel cornered. All because of the way he looks at me.

What's worse, what's maddening and suffocating, is that I love it. I fucking want this. The way he looks at me is addicting; it's freeing in more ways than one.

I can't chicken out. I won't.

I nod my head once, as his fingers trail up to my throat and his hand wraps around my neck, his light touch feeling much rougher than he's being with me. I tilt my head, as his grip moves to my chin. He just barely brushes his lips against mine. It's a soft kiss that leaves me wanting more. I keep my eyes closed, I stay as still as can be as he hovers them so close and whispers, "I want to kiss you."

"Kiss me," I whimper, a pathetic plea, or maybe one of strength. My head feels so clouded, it's hard to know what's driving me. Raw, primal instinct or desperation. Perhaps a lethal cocktail of both.

He pulls away just slightly, but I don't let him get far. I take a half step closer to him, my breast brushing against his shirt and I crush my lips into his. I need him. I need this.

He's quick to wrap his arms around me and pull my body up against his own. The faint noises of the night surround us and they seem to get louder as my breathing gets heavier. His lips travel down my throat and I throw my head back. It doesn't escape me that we're out in the open, but I find it too difficult to care. I may have been tipsy from the alcohol before, but in this moment, I'm drunk with lust.

"I want to fuck you, Jules." Mason practically growls. He pulls me into him suddenly and forces a gasp from me as he nips my earlobe. "I want to make you cum so hard you forget everything." I moan as his lips trail down my neck.

My nipples harden and my back arches as my pussy heats. "The only thing you need to remember is my name," he whispers into my ear, his hands roaming further down my ass and waist until his bare skin touches mine. "Just my name and what I've done to you tonight."

I tilt my head back and everything he's saying is exactly what I need to hear. "Yes," I whisper into the soft breeze that cools my exposed hot skin.

"Only tonight," he whispers so low, I nearly miss it. My fingers slip under his shirt, so I can feel his bare skin too and it triggers him to pull away from me. Just slightly, only so he can look into my eyes, but I grip him harder. I'm afraid to lose what he's offering me.

I want him. I want his promise.

I want to forget and feel alive again.

"Yes," I whisper and then press my lips to his, moving a hand to the back of his head, my fingers spearing through his thick hair as his tongue strokes mine and he lifts me up into his arms by my ass.

I gasp from the sudden movement and wrap my legs around his waist. I can't say no now. I can't and won't. He takes the opportunity to leave open-mouthed kisses down my neck and torture my deprived body.

Every doubt leaves me. All I need is to be held by this man. Fucked by him, and ruined by him.

I come alive for him, every nerve ending on fire, ready to burst into a flame so hot I can't control myself. My fingers dig into his shoulders, my nails scratching along his shirt and wishing it were skin.

The pleasure is so intense already. It's nearly too much. I want to pull away because the inevitable drop from this high is going to shatter me. I'm all too aware of it, but I can't help myself.

He never stops kissing me as he balances me in one strong arm and unlocks the door. He never sets me down until he has me on his bed.

And he never gives me the chance to think about anything but the desire threatening to destroy me.

I bounce slightly on the bed and it throws me off balance, but I don't have time to recover. He practically rips at my dress, desperate to have me bared to him. I reach behind me, unclasping my bra as he pulls the lace down my body. His fingers loop around my thong and takes it along with the black dress.

My heels fall to the floor, each thudding and mixing with the sound of my heart racing. I'm given a moment, only a quick moment as he pulls his shirt over his head. But instead of thinking about what I'm doing, instead of falling for the self-doubt and fears, I'm mesmerized by the rippling of his muscles and then by the girth and rigidity of his cock as he shoves his pants off.

It happened so fast. Like a whirlwind of chaos, that only surrounded the two of us. The mattress groans with his weight as I prop myself up on my elbows. He slides between my legs, not asking me to spread my thighs for him. My body behaves naturally, opening up for him as if he was meant to be there. As if my movements were controlled by his desires.

My heart beats so hard, it feels like it's trying to get away from me. His hard, hot body pushes down against mine and I can't breathe. But I don't want to.

My head turns to one side and then the other, feeling the cool sheet beneath my cheek as the head of his dick brushes against my slick folds.

"You're so wet for me," he says and Mason's voice is a mixture of wonder and reverence. I try to move my head again, but he captures my lips with his and suddenly pushes his cock deep inside of me, all the way to the hilt in one swift stroke.

I scream out, my neck arching and my back bowing as he stills and gives me a moment to adjust to his size. My heart squeezes in my chest, but then, he moves.

Not just moves. He fucks me with a punishing force. The bed slams against the wall with each thrust. He kisses me as though he's breathing the air from my lungs. He pins me down and takes everything from me, forcing me higher and higher, all while giving me everything I never knew I needed.

It's not until I'm left panting and recovering from waves of pleasure that I start to question what I've done. But it's so late and I'm so exhausted. I forget it all, except what he's done to me and give in to sleep.

CHAPTER 9

Mason

The fire roars. The flames, they grow.
The light it calls, but this you know.
You shouldn't touch it, you shouldn't play.
The flames are tempting, but you will pay.
It's meant to burn, soot black, smoke white.
You escape with a kiss, mesmerized by the light.
You think you're done, the fire's gone out.
But it's not done with you, it will never be without.

LAST NIGHT WAS STUPID. Such a juvenile word, but I can't think of anything better. Fucking stupid.

I'll blame it on the alcohol. A low groan travels up my throat as I move away from the floor-to-ceiling window in my office. The hustle and bustle of the streets below is what drives me to keep moving. This city never sleeps, and the work never ends.

Last night was about taking a moment to unwind from the shitshow my life has become. From my father, the arrogant prick and criminal that he is. The lines separating right and wrong have blurred, and the awareness of just how ruthless my father is has never hurt me more.

That's what it really is. *Pain.* Coming to the realization that your father's a disgusting excuse for a human being and should be locked away behind bars is... difficult to handle. What's worse is when you're tied into his bullshit.

I sink into the leather desk chair. Unlike my father's office, traditional and smelling of polished wood and old books, my office is the opposite. It's airy and open with the model of our newest development in the very center.

That's what started all this shit. A celebration for my company's first suburban development. No more apartments downtown. We're ready to take over and start creeping into uncharted territories. I'm a fucking idiot for thinking this would change things between my father and me. I really thought things would be different. I'd attributed the tense relationship with him to my own doing. I was a rebellious child with pent-up anger over my mother's death. Born into this black tie bullshit with no choice or say.

I was always supposed to act right. Always supposed to say the right thing, stand the right way, behave and pay attention. Well, I didn't fucking want to. I crack my neck, remembering the fights I started. A smile kicks my lips up. Four boarding schools and hefty donations from my father still couldn't keep me in line.

Working in construction was just another "fuck you" to my father.

Higher education? Fuck that. I wanted a physical job... but it didn't last for long. I'm just not made to work for someone else. So I started Grays Homes with Liam nearly three years ago. He had the schooling, and I had the designs. I didn't think it'd be this successful, or grow so quickly. So much so that I ran out of cash flow, and so did he. We did what we had to in order to keep growing and taking advantage of the momentum we had. I took out loan after loan, investing in myself and I'd do it all over again.

But I wish I hadn't agreed when my father came to me and offered to invest in me, too.

Just having him backing me made everything easier and run smoother. I knew it was too good to be true.

He just wanted to hold it over my head. He wanted to *own* me. I narrow my eyes at the model in the center of the room. It's all because of this. Now I'm in debt, I owe more than I'm worth and everything's hanging in the balance. This one project is the key. I should cancel it all now that I know the truth, but that would mean bankruptcy and more people than just myself being affected. Liam and all of our employees and contractors would lose everything.

I pull my eyes back to the computer screen, back to all the bills that have been paid. Everything's moving accordingly, but only because of the income from my father's loan.

I fucking need him. If I turned him in...

I run my hand over my face, knowing I'm just as much of a fucking prick. I don't deserve to breathe the same air as someone as sweet as Jules.

The thought of her shy smile and innocent looks... God, it does something to me. The guilt and anger are minimal compared to my desire. I want to feel her again. I want to get lost in her touch, fascinated by the fact that I do the same to her.

I can make it all better.

She has no idea how fucked up it is. My father would, but not nearly to the same extent.

He may be a piece of shit and deserve to live behind bars, but if the world knew what I'd done, they would think the same of me.

I click the mouse to light up the screen as it goes dim once again. I can't think; I can't focus.

As my temples throb and irritation grows, I think back to last night. Back to Jules.

Out of every possible way for this morning to start, I never guessed she'd sneak out.

I imagined how we'd leave things over and over again while I watched her sleep, her long hair a beautiful halo on the pillow. She looked so peaceful and beautiful.

I'll never forgive myself. I couldn't get over how fucked up it was. How selfish of me. But it turned out to be everything I wanted, and more. *It was fucking worth it.*

As she slept, exhausted and spent from the raw fuck, my fingers longed to travel along her curves. My dick was still hard for more.

Staring at her lush lips, the visions of her eyes shut tight, her head thrown back, and her mouth parted with soft, strangled moans spilling between them were etched in my memory. It was the sexiest fucking thing I've ever seen. Jules was a woman utterly in rapture from what I was doing to her. She was completely at my mercy, and I know she loved every minute.

I tugged the blankets over myself and lay there watching her, debating how I'd end it in the morning. I could crave her more than anything, but it was over. And it never should have started to begin with. As I thought about exactly what to say to ease the sting, I watched her steady breathing and my lungs filled with her sweet scent.

Just once more. I should have spread her legs and taken her again. Had I known that I'd wake up alone, I would have.

I sit back in my leather seat, letting out an aggravated sigh as I watch the security tape again. She slipped out, only leaving a note behind. I watch in amusement as she keeps looking up from the small Post-it she'd found on my kitchen counter. The pen never even touched the paper for a full two minutes as she contemplated what to write.

She's lost and confused. She doesn't even know what she wants.

But I do.

I move the sticky side of the Post-it from my middle finger to my pointer and back again mindlessly.

Thank you.

If last night was more than just last night...

I trace the curves of her letters; it's a feminine script. She was made to tempt men. I'm convinced of it. Everything from the soft sighs to the way she carries herself are clear signs.

It's as if she was designed to lure me in unknowingly.

Even the way she's written her phone number. Each gentle sweep makes my fingers yearn to punch in the numbers on my phone.

Weakness. Stupidity.

Last night was a mistake. I don't have to call her. I don't owe her anything, and I'm fairly sure she doesn't expect a damn thing either.

Why does that bother me even more?

The sticky note continues to move from finger to finger. I know I shouldn't call her. Nothing good can come from this.

My eyes trail back to her message. Again I stare at her phone number.

Selfish. So fucking selfish.

That's the problem though, isn't it? I just don't give a damn about anyone else. The thought is what strengthens my resolve. It's all going to come crumbling down around me soon. I deserve to enjoy what little time I have left.

CHAPTER 10

*J*ulia

Deep breaths, it'll be okay.
We're done with yesterday.
It doesn't matter, hold back the tears.
Ignore the hurt, ignore the fears.
It's okay, there's nothing wrong.
Don't let go, just hold on strong.

THE WATER TRICKLES slowly from the spout of the iron faucet. I grip the side of the claw foot porcelain tub, the water splashing slightly in the otherwise silent room as I get comfortable. Then I rest my cheek against the cool, hard porcelain and watch it drip.

The water's practically lukewarm by now, but I don't want to get out. My wet hair clings to my skin and I sink in further, letting the water rise up to my neck. My legs sway side to side, and the water still drips.

Last night... it was a mistake. And this morning, I close my eyes and bring my hands up to my face, that was a mistake, too. There's nothing in etiquette class about leaving your one-night stand.

My throat feels raw as I take in a breath, remembering how last night felt. His hands on my body, his chest against mine as he rocked in and out of me, mercilessly, ruthlessly.

I've never... I swallow thickly, hating that I'm even comparing what happened to what I had with my husband. I feel like a bitch riddled with guilt, but I just let myself fall into the water, as if I can wash it all away.

No amount of time spent in this tub will clean away the sins of last night.

One good thing's come of it though. The words are flowing through me so easily. All I've done since I've been home is write. I shouldn't be happy about that, and I shouldn't feel like this.

The pain in my chest though, the way my heart feels tight and my lungs too squished to breathe quite right, that's because I don't regret it.

I feel guilty that I don't feel guilty. How does that even make sense?

Ping. My phone dings and I groan, squeezing my eyes tight. I must've been more than a bit tipsy last night to let Sue act as my conscience. She won't leave me alone. There were way too many fucking texts for her to have gone home with anyone herself last night.

I woke up this morning to a string of texts from her. Lots of *Please tell me he didn't kill you* messages, and a series of apologies if he did. She thinks she's funny. I thought I was doing a good thing by letting her know I was still in fact alive and unharmed, but all that did was open a floodgate of questions.

I can't help the way my lips beg me to smile and the way my heart flutters. Sue's having a good time teasing me. I push my big toe up into the spout as I slip deeper into the water and rest my head back.

Ping. My phone goes off again. I turn my head to the right, to where my towel and phone are sitting on the marble bench.

I can only imagine what she wants to know this time.

"I can't hide in here forever," I mutter under my breath, blowing the water away and finally lifting myself out of the comfort of the bath. I lean down and pull the plug, letting the cool air hit my heated skin.

It was nice while it lasted and after last night, it did my body good to relax in here. As I lean over to grab the towel, my pussy aches again with a slight twinge of pain. It's a good hurt though, the kind that lets you know you've been properly fucked. I laugh slightly into the towel and dry off my body, then work on patting my hair dry. My feet patter against the black and white penny tile floor.

The bathroom matches the estate's classic interior. Every accent and piece of décor reflects the timing of when the house was built. There are a few modern pieces, but they only accentuate the beauty of the classic architecture. It's expensive to maintain, but the beauty is unmatched.

I continue towel drying my long hair as the memories of renovating the house come to me one by one. The bit of happiness I'd claimed only moments ago seems to vanish.

Jace and I got into so many fights over this damn tile. I can see him standing in front of the mirror, glaring at me for being stubborn. It's my family's house though. This isn't an Anderson estate. We both knew I was far more well off than he ever was. The steamy glass can't hide the past. I can hear his voice; I can see it all like it was just yesterday.

But it was years ago, and he's never coming back.

Ping. This time when the phone goes off, I can't help but want to cling to whatever Sue's sending me. I take a seat on the bench, wincing as my sore bottom sits against the hard marble and pick up the damn phone.

But it's not her.

Well, this last message isn't.

I have three from Sue, all wanting to know details about what I did with Mason last night. I roll my eyes and let out a small snort at her question about size.

By the looks of him, he should be packing... but I'm going to guess he's only four inches. Am I right?

She cracks me up. She's been sending me this shit all day. Anything to get me talking.

Nope, only three, I type back just to give her something to laugh about. She deserves it. Without all these messages and prodding I'm not sure how I would have handled this on my own.

I click over to the other message and my heart does an odd flip in my chest. Like it can't function for just a moment. Maybe it's shock and disbelief, or maybe it's fear? I'm not sure, but either way, I'm struck by the fact that Mason messaged me at all. I was sure that sneaking out the way I did would have sealed the deal between the two of us.

I wasn't even sure if I should leave my phone number. I imagine he was relieved to find his drunken one-night stand gone, and I didn't want him to feel obligated to call me.

At the same time, I desperately wanted him to call.

Not because of him. It's not that I'm clinging to having a relationship at all. I just... I liked the way he made me... I don't know what the right word is. The way nothing else mattered when I was with him. How it all slipped away, and I didn't have to focus on anything but him. Mostly because he was only focused on me.

I want more of that. I need it. I bite down on my bottom lip and read the message.

It's not a question, and it's not a hello or an admonishment for leaving him.

I want to see you again. Blue Hill. 8 p.m. tonight.

I blink a few times at the message, and then a bit of anger starts to surface. He's so fucking presumptuous. As if I have nothing better to do than meet up with him.

I don't, if I'm being honest with myself. I haven't got a damn thing to do, other than write, which can wait, and everything in me wants to meet up with him. I lose a little bit of the fight in me at the thought, but still. This isn't happening like this.

I look down at the message again and the second read through only pisses me off even more.

Maybe I want a good fuck too, and by maybe I mean I fucking need it, but I'm not a goddamn call girl. Last night was something out of my realm.

Busy. I type in the word and hit send without even thinking, letting my high and mighty attitude lead me. But as soon as it pops up on the screen, oh fuck I wish I could take it back.

My head falls back, and I groan in aggravation. I should have just said yes. After all, I'm using him too, aren't I? I'm so busy staring at the ceiling and cursing myself that when my phone pings in my hand, I jump slightly.

Are you now?

His response should piss me off, but it makes me smile. I can just imagine the teasing way he would say it. Like he knows exactly why I responded like that. I smirk and bite the inside of my cheek as I text back.

Maybe I am.

His response is immediate. *You are now. Blue Hill. 8 p.m.*

My shoulders straighten, and I can't help but feel like this is some kind of test. Like a battle of wills between us. And I have no intention of losing.

Busy.

I hit send and wait for his response. I'm just staring at the screen and listening to the blood rush through my ears as the phone marks the message as read.

There's no immediate message back, and I start to question my position. I don't want to be alone tonight. I know it's pathetic, but I'm so tired of being lonely, lying in bed at night, staring at where Jace used to sleep.

I take in a heavy breath when Mason doesn't message me back. It's probably best that I don't see Mason tonight anyway. I've never been alone before, and I'm too tempted to cling to him already. I push my hair back and try to decide if I should convince Sue to go out tonight. I'm sure she would if only I asked. Any of the girls would, and I fucking love them for it.

The phone pings in my hand and like a bitch in heat, I'm quick to read what he's said.

You win. Your call.

I bite the inside of my cheek and sway slightly as I write my response.

CHAPTER 11

Mason

Don't breathe, the truth is baiting.
Don't move, the end is waiting.
Don't blink, you've started it all.
Don't mourn, you're set up to fall.

"So who is she?" Liam asks me from his office as I'm on my way out. He leans out of the doorway, both hands on the doorframe and smirks at me.

"Who?" I ask, turning my back to him again so I can lock up my office. It's a habit of mine. No one has a key but me. I've got fifteen employees here who come and go throughout the day, but my office is only for me.

"The chick you hooked up with last night." I test the doorknob, making sure it's locked, and toss my keys into my pocket. I'm just heading across the street to the sandwich shop. I won't be long, which is good because I want to have all these numbers run by the time I need to leave for Blue Hill.

When I turn back around, Liam's got his arms crossed and he's leaning against the door, waiting for me like I owe him some sort of explanation.

"None of your business," I say and smirk back at him.

"Oh shit," he says and his brow furrows. "You really did hook up with someone last night?" he asks me with disbelief. Liam's always been a talker. He doesn't seem to mind my demeanor as much as everyone else. Give him enough time and he can have an entire conversation by himself, so maybe the two of us were just meant to be friends.

He pushes off the doorframe and says, "I was going to give you shit for leaving me hanging last night."

"Just didn't want to be alone last night," I tell him honestly. "Better her company than yours," I say with a grin, trying to lighten the mood.

"So are we going to go over it tonight then?" he asks me.

"Go over what?"

"What our investor said at the meeting you had without me yesterday." By investor, he means my father.

"It wasn't about Grays Homes." I take a few steps down the hall, closer to his office. Mine's the largest, and in the very back. Liam's is catty-corner to mine and the only other office in here. Across from his office is the boardroom, which is currently empty and really only ever used for sales pitches and end of quarter wrap-ups.

"Oh." Liam seems genuinely taken by surprise. His face says everything though, and it's clear he wants to ask me a million fucking questions. Why was my father so insistent on meeting with me? Why did he come in here over and over and finally force my hand?

"It's been a bit tense for the last few months between us," I admit, keeping my voice low enough so it's just the two of us in this conversation. I know Margaret, our secretary, is right down the hall and close enough to hear if we talk loud enough.

"Few months?" he asks me.

I stare at him, feeling my expression hardening. I stopped talking to my father a while ago. I know this is a necessary evil. I'm caught between wanting to do what's right, and knowing for sure that I'd be doing the right thing. So instead of acting, I've been avoiding him every chance I got.

It worked my entire life up until now. Until he told me what I already knew, confirming it and forcing me to face the truth.

"Don't worry about it." I give him a tight smile. "It's got nothing to do with the business."

"And what about you?" he asks. "I can't be worried about you?"

I shake my head. "I'm fine."

"Yeah, you keep saying that," he says then turns his shoulder like he's going to head back into his office as the phone rings.

"Go get it," I say and nod past him toward the inside of his office. "I'm just picking up a Reuben."

"Alright," he mutters and starts to head into his office, but before I make it another two steps he's popping his head outside of the door again. "Will you get me a Coke?"

I look over my shoulder at him, the sounds of everyone else working getting louder and louder. "Yeah." I don't break my stride as I head down the hall. Our company owns this floor of the Rising Falls Building; it's a tall office building that's made for businesses just like ours. The second I stepped in here I knew this was where I wanted to work. There's clear glass everywhere. So much natural light and the views of the city give constant inspiration.

Even the cubicles have plexiglass walls.

"Out to lunch?" Margaret asks as I walk past her.

"I'll be right back," I say and nod, again not breaking my stride and head past all my employees to the elevator.

"Yes, sir," Margaret answers with a light-hearted tone. I've never seen that woman not smile. It's as if being our secretary is the highlight of her day. She's damn good at what she does, too. At first I was opposed to letting anyone step in and take control of scheduling and inventory, but as we grew, I just couldn't handle it all.

I push the button for the elevator and when I hear the ping, I'm reminded of Jules' text. The irritation and anger that surfaced from thinking about my father nearly vanishes.

Just the thought of what was going through her mind when she texted me back makes me smile. She's a testy little thing. I didn't expect that. There's more to Miss Summers than I thought there was, and I'm definitely intrigued.

I check my Rolex as the elevator dings and the doors slowly open. There's no one inside so I walk right in and hit the button for the ground floor. Only six hours until dinner.

My chest feels tight, and the small smile leaves me. It's fucked up in so many ways, but she'll never know. I'll make sure she never finds out.

CHAPTER 12

Julia

They don't understand,
How it takes away the pain.
To feel and be felt.
To heat the blood in your veins.
They'll watch and they'll judge,
Although they'd do it, too.
But the guilt's not from them.
It's coming from you.

PASTEL PINK MACARONS, and crystal chandeliers. I love this place. It's a tiny shop and the treats are too damn expensive for what they are, but it's the vibe I love. I scoot my silver stool closer to the small round table and peel the cupcake wrapper as I listen to Suzette.

"I just want to know every last detail," she says with barely contained joy. Kat looks between the two of us and hasn't touched a thing on the etched tray in the center of the table. I know there's something there that would make her smile, but she's not interested.

I can feel both sets of their eyes on me, but I don't look up. It's too pretty in this little shop to feel this damn anxious. My eyes settle on the tall crystal flute of pink champagne and I take a quick sip, tilting my head up to look at the carved tin ceiling. Everything in here is pink, silver, shiny and new. So pretty to look at, but useless in saving Kat's attitude.

"How could you not tell us?" she says, and her voice is low. She's still standing, her purse on the stool and I don't think she has any intention of sitting down in the least. She's pissed. "That's what I really don't get."

Her eyes are boring into me, and the disappointment in her voice makes my appetite for all things sweet and scrumptious vanish.

I knew this was coming. You can't just take off from Katerina Thompson and not have her chew you out later.

"It wasn't meant as an insult," I start to answer her. It's not like I was trying to upset her, and she should at least know that for a fact.

"It's because you would have stopped her," Sue says before shoving half of a tiny cupcake into her mouth and biting it right down the middle. She has no shame and gives Kat the answer as if it's obvious. And I mean, come on, it is.

"No shit I would have stopped her." Her wrath is directed at Sue now, and to be honest, I'm grateful. Sue doesn't give a fuck. Literally, not a single fuck given. She stares Kat right in the eyes as she pushes the other half of the cupcake into her mouth with her pointer.

"It's not that I was really thinking," I say. There's a small plea in my voice for Kat to just calm down.

"Of course you weren't," Kat snaps but immediately looks like she wants to take it back.

"Oh hush," Sue says easily and then nods at me. "Good for you for going out and dusting off those cobwebs." I snort a small laugh, and my shoulders shake from it. "He's cute, too."

"He better be," Kat says beneath her breath, pulling out a bottle of water from her oversized Michael Kors hobo bag.

Sue rolls her eyes as she asks, "You gonna track him down and beat the shit out of him if he isn't?" A smile forces its way onto my face and I try my damnedest to make it go away, but it's not happening. Kat glares at Sue for a moment before returning to her water and taking a sip.

"So, your first one-night stand... how does it feel?" Sue asks.

I could write a damn book on the shit I'm feeling right now. The guilt and regret, the anxiety. But the other things, the bit of liveliness and... is it pride? Is that what it is? Knowing that I was wanted and desired like *that*? And that he still wants me? Yeah, that's a bit of pride, which is odd to be feeling over something like this.

"He texted me this morning," I confess and sway a little in my seat, picking at the hem of the tablecloth. "He wants to go out tonight."

Sue's mouth drops open as her eyes go wide. "Really?" She grins in slow motion and then makes a face as she wipes her fingertips on her napkin.

"What's that for?" I ask her.

Sue shrugs and replies, "Nothing."

"That's not a nothing look," I tell her right back, "That's a something look."

"You must've been good." Sue pops a piece of macaron into her mouth and smiles wide. The tiered tray was filled with an assortment when we got here, but it's almost empty except for the big cupcakes now.

My mouth opens some, and I have to force it back shut. By the heat on my cheeks, I imagine I'm beet red. Yeah, it's definitely pride.

"So what'd you tell him?" Kat asks.

I'm embarrassed that I said I was busy and then said yes to the exact time and location he said originally, so I just cut to the chase. "I said yes."

"You said yes to a date for tonight that was asked today?" Kat asks in a tone that makes it seem like my answer could be the difference between life and death.

"I did," I answer slowly as Sue claps her hands and leans her head back with laughter. She's so loud that a few customers in line at the counter look over at her.

"I love her. This is just too good to be true." Sue's smile just gets bigger and bigger until she spots the last tiny cupcake.

"I don't understand." I look between the two of them to find out what I've done wrong.

"You never say yes to a date on the day of." My lips purse as Kat crosses her arms and looks at me like I should know better.

"Well, I told him no at first." That's my only defense. And really, do I give a fuck?

"But then you said yes," Kat clarifies, and I nod in return.

"I just wanted to go out." That weird feeling in my chest comes back. The one that makes me feel like I'm sick. Like all of this is wrong and I should feel guilty about it.

"With a stranger!" It's Kat this time that gets the attention of the customers, and between the two of them I wish I could just leave.

"Well, not quite," Sue interrupts, "they did fuck."

Kat grabs her head in her hands and looks down at the ground groaning, "Oh my God."

Her response makes me feel like complete and utter shit. "Just leave me alone. Seriously," I grumble and shove the tiny white plate away from me, hating that I feel like this. That my friends are making me feel like this. "I haven't gone out in-" my throat gets tight, and my breathing picks up. I refuse to fucking cry right now, to cry over this shit. I won't do it. I won't be made to feel guilty about it either. Not more than I already do.

"I didn't plan this, Kat." I point at my chest for emphasis and stare into her green eyes. The only emotion in her expression is regret. "You don't think I feel like..." I swallow the sharp lump in my throat and try to will away all the shit emotions.

"No, no," Sue speaks up and gets off her stool to get closer to me. "Don't get all upset over this." She shakes her head as she tries to calm me down, but it's not working.

"You too!" I yell at her, and I don't even know why I yelled. Yes, the questions are irritating the fuck out of me, but at least Sue isn't trying to make me feel like shit.

She raises both her hands defensively. "Hey, I'm not the one slut-shaming."

Kat whips her head to Sue and says sharply, "It's not slut-shaming." Everyone in the entire fucking shop is looking at us at this point. "He could have been a murderer!" she practically shrieks.

"Oh, calm down!" Sue looks genuinely pissed. "She was safe. I knew where she was," Sue talks more to Kat than me, "and she was fine." She emphasizes the word "fine" then slips off her stool, grabbing her purse off the table. "I actually have to get back to the office."

I take a sip of my champagne, but there's practically nothing in it. Fucking figures.

"You have fun tonight," Sue says with a wink, like the last five minutes didn't happen. I give her a small smile back and kiss her cheek before she moves to the other side.

Maddie's not coming to this little cupcake brunch, so it's just me and Kat now. I don't like the feeling that I need armor to have a quick chat with one of my closest friends. I bite the inside of my cheek as I watch Sue leave completely nonplussed, the bells above the door jingling as I shift on the stool.

I know Kat's looking at me, waiting for me to say something. Why do I feel like I owe her an apology? I let out a quick breath and face her, my shoulders square and my heart out on my sleeve. It's always there; that's how I've always lived my life.

"Kat, look-"

"Nope," she cuts me off and holds up her hand. "It's fine. Last night was fine. Tonight is fine." She nods her head once, moving the purse from on top of her stool to the one Sue was sitting on. She finally takes a seat, tugging her black pencil skirt down. Her white blouse is nearly see through, but she still looks professional. She always appears on top of everything.

I start to explain my position. "I know it upset you for me to leave and not tell you." I lean forward, putting my hand closer to her on the table.

"I think I overreacted," Kat says not looking at me at first, but then she lifts her eyes to mine. "It really is okay, and I'm not trying to make you feel bad." Her words come out with sincerity, and it surprises me how much I needed that. "Or slut-shame you or anything like that."

"Thank you," I reply and my voice cracks some and I roll my eyes, looking for my glass, but again finding it empty. I run my fingertips down the stem, feeling overwhelmed with guilt even though Kat's told me she's not shaming me.

She isn't why I feel guilty.

"Am I a bad person?" I ask Kat, finally pulling my eyes from the empty flute to look at her.

"No," she answers with sad eyes, taking my hand in both of hers.

"Honestly," she hesitates and it makes me that much more nervous. "I'm surprised after everything that happened..."

You must really live in a shit world when your closest friend says "everything that happened" and you need clarification on which specific thing she's talking about.

I'm quiet waiting for her to finish, but she doesn't.

"Just tell me that he's not going to make you miss your deadline." Kat's trying to ease the tension. She's my editor, and this manuscript is due in two weeks.

A smile grows on my face, but it's not genuine in the least. I know for a fact I'm going to miss that deadline. She doesn't need to know that though. "He won't." I shake my head cheerfully, my hair swishing against my shoulders.

"Okay then," she says and raises her brows and finally picks up a cupcake. Kat goes for a large cupcake with hot pink icing and an Oreo stuck in the center. "Please tell me you're at least using condoms until you get back on the pill or something."

I know she meant for that to be funny, but when I give her some side-eye and shrug, she practically chokes on that damn Oreo.

CHAPTER 13

Mason

So close you can touch her,
Delicate and sweet.
You need her, you crave her,
To hide your deceit.
Be gentle and coaxing,
You can't let her know.
If she finds out the truth,
Out the door she will go.

BLUE HILL always dims the lights in the evening. That, along with the soothing sounds of the water flowing down the river rock wall, and the lit candle on the table, all makes the tone of the evening extremely romantic. The other guests are quiet, so the only really sound is the clinking of silverware and glasses as I wait for Jules to walk through the doors.

My fingertips brush over the silver tines of my salad fork as I stare straight ahead toward the entrance and maître d'. Guests have come and gone since I sat down twenty minutes ago, each one catching my attention and disappointing me. I glance down at my watch again; she still has five minutes until she's late.

I make a habit of being early, but I'm regretting it this time. Every minute that passes makes me more and more eager to leave. Curiosity is the only thing keeping me here in my seat. The door opens, and the soft cadence of heels clicking on the slate floor reverberates in the room.

She's here. Jules slips her grey wool pea coat off as she walks in, and then places it in her arms as she walks to the maître d'. I stand before she can utter a word and button my suit jacket as I walk toward her. I'm only a few tables down and she sees me just as the man asks her if she has a reservation.

"She's with me." My voice comes out deep, confident... and possessive. As she turns toward my voice, the hem of her plum-colored dress swirls around her thighs. It's tight around her ass and waist, showing off her curves and reminding me how she looked beneath me last night.

"Of course," the maître d' nods.

"Thank you," Jules says sweetly, giving him a soft smile and looking back at me. It's only a quick glance before a blush rises to her cheeks and she tucks a lock of hair behind her ear and walks toward me.

She has that shy elegance about her, but there's more to her than that. I want to dig a little deeper, if for nothing more than curiosity's sake.

I gesture toward the table, pulling out her chair for her like a gentleman. It's not in my nature, but I have enough manners to impress a woman at least.

"I'm surprised you wanted to see me again," Jules says as I take my own seat.

Before I can respond she adds, "Thank you, by the way." Her eyes flicker from mine to the candle. I don't miss how she takes a few glances around us as if she's searching for someone.

I nod my head once easily, setting the napkin in my lap and giving her a moment to get comfortable. The waiter quickly pours her a glass of water.

"Good evening. May I start you off with something to drink?" The young man squares his shoulders and waits, holding a glass pitcher at attention. He's dressed in a crisp white button-down and dark grey slacks that match his thin tie.

"A bourbon for me please," I answer him and look back at Jules. Her slender neck and shoulders are on display. The way the thin straps of her dress lay across the very edge of her shoulders makes me want to pull them down. A simple thin silver necklace sits right in the dip of her collarbone with the word "happy" etched in the middle. It's the only piece of jewelry she's wearing. The fact there's no ring on her finger doesn't escape me. I'm tempted to ask her about it, but I don't.

"A glass of chardonnay, please?" she says.

"Right away," the waiter says and nods, leaving us alone and once again Jules squirms uncomfortably. I love her nervousness and how she has a habit of tucking her hair behind her ear. It only adds to her innocence.

"No tequila?" I play with her.

She huffs a small laugh and rolls her eyes. "No," she says as she unfolds the napkin in her lap, smoothing it out. "No tequila tonight."

I shrug, waiting for those soft baby blue eyes to look back up at me. "I didn't mind the tequila," I whisper across the table. There's not a damn thing dirty that I've said, but she still blushes. There's an attraction between us that's undeniable. It's easy and carefree. But the air is tense as she looks to her left again and then back to me.

She hesitates to say something, but then changes her mind and clears her throat as she picks up the menu.

She starts talking without looking at me. "I've never done anything like this."

"Like what?" I ask her.

"Like, seeing someone."

"Is that what we're doing?" I ask, slightly amused. "Seeing each other?"

She puts her menu down and looks at me with a serious expression. "I have no idea." The sincere answer and complete honesty in her voice forces a rough laugh from my chest. I was only teasing her, but she's too sweet and sincere for me to get a rise out of her.

"You can laugh all you want, but I have no clue what's going on." She picks her menu back up and says, "I'm just along for the ride, Mr. Thatcher."

"Is that so?" I ask playfully and pick up my glass of water as the waiter comes back over to us, setting down my drink and then hers.

"It is," she says absently, smiling into her glass and taking a sip of the white wine. She closes her eyes and lets out a barely audible soft moan of satisfaction. My cock starts hardening as I remember last night, and the same sweet sound slipping from her lips as I thrust into her over and over again.

She's completely oblivious.

"So what changed in your plans?" I ask as she eyes the menu again. I don't bother picking mine up. I know exactly what I'll have.

A short, feminine laugh makes her shoulders shake as she pulls her long blonde hair over her shoulder and then brushes it back again. She shrugs and then finally answers, "I thought this would be better than what I had planned."

Bullshit. I can tell she's lying from a mile away.

"And what did you have planned before?"

She takes a sip of wine and then answers, "Writing."

"Writing?" I ask.

"I like to go to Central Park to write," she says, slipping her hands into her lap and leaning forward.

"Are you a journalist?"

"No," she says and shakes her head, "I'm an author." She takes a sip of wine again and I watch as she fiddles with the stem and continues. "I'm not well known or anything. I just write poetry." She tries to wave off her insecurity and then adds, "It doesn't really make much money, but it's the career I chose."

She's already justifying her life, and I don't like it. She should be proud of herself.

"I think that's wonderful. It takes a lot of work and diligence to write a novel of poetry."

Her eyes light up, and she visibly relaxes as she says in a delicate voice, "Thank you."

"Who's your favorite poet?" I ask.

"Robert Frost," she answers quickly. "Hands down."

"I've read a bit of Frost." It's true albeit years and years ago in grade school, and I'm pretty sure I hated every minute I was forced to read it. It doesn't matter though, because my remark makes her calm and that sweet smile comes back.

I clear my throat, smoothing the napkin on my lap and trying to remember what Mrs. Harper, my favorite teacher in tenth grade taught me. "Poetry is when an emotion has found its thought," I look into her eyes and try to say the second part correctly, "and the thought has found words.' I believe it was Frost who said that." Her entire demeanor changes to one of surprise and ease. I'm shocked that I remembered it myself.

A sweet smile looks back at me. It's amazing how something so small can make her genuinely happy. She nods and says, "Yes, I do believe you're right."

The moment between us is filled with a comfortable silence as we each take a sip of our drinks.

"So what do you do?" she asks.

"I'm a property developer," I answer shortly. I don't think she has any idea of the connections. I don't intend to lie to her, but I don't need to give her anything to help her connect the dots.

"Oh, in the city?"

"Brooklyn mostly, although we're currently under contract with the city to renovate and rebuild some properties in Manhattan."

"Oh wow, what's that like?"

"Being a developer?" I've never had anyone ask me that before. "It's... challenging at times, and it pisses me off most days." I smirk at her as she laughs into her glass at my answer. "Isn't that what all jobs are like though?"

She nods her head, setting the glass down but then her expression changes.

"I'm not sure I should be doing this," she tells me with her forehead scrunched.

"Doing what?"

"This," she says and gestures between the two of us.

"We aren't doing anything."

Her eyes narrow and I ignore the accusatory stare, picking up my bourbon and taking an easy drink of it. It burns just right on the way down, leaving a trail of heat in its wake.

"I just want to feed you," I say in a voice that I hope comes out somewhat innocent.

"And fuck me," she says so softly and with a roughness I haven't heard from that sexy voice of hers. I look up, daring her to blush, to be embarrassed by it, but she only stares back with desire in her baby blue eyes.

"Yes, and fuck you," I admit. It doesn't go unnoticed that she clenches her thighs. "You want that, don't you?"

"I'm not sure I should be fucking you," she says simply, but with a firm resolve in her voice. My heart beats in a way that makes my chest feel tight. Like there's not quite enough room for it to beat again.

"Are you fucking someone else?" I ask her. My knuckles brush against the white tablecloth as my hands start to clench into fists. I stop them and try to keep my body from showing what I'm really feeling. She better not be fucking anyone else.

She loses the conviction in her voice when she answers, "No."

"Then why not?" I ask her, glancing at the waiter as he starts walking toward us.

"Because-" Jules stops as soon as she notices him. She puts on a fake smile that doesn't reach her eyes and waits patiently for him to address her.

"Are you ready for me to take your order?" he asks me, but I gesture to Jules, taking another drink to settle my irritation.

"For you, miss?"

"May I have the herb-grilled salmon, please?" She passes her menu to him and rests her hands in her lap, giving him her full attention. Meanwhile I can't take my eyes off of her and thinking about why the fuck she thinks she shouldn't be seeing me.

"Are the grilled vegetables alright with that?" he asks her. It pisses me off how she smiles back and answers, "Yes, that's perfect." It's irrational, but I just want to be alone with her.

The waiter scribbles in the notepad in his hand and then turns toward me.

"Sirloin, medium rare. Vegetables are fine." I preemptively answer his unasked question, still staring at Jules. The waiter takes the hint, nodding once and immediately leaving us.

"You were saying?" I ask her, picking up my bourbon.

"I-" She hesitates, sensing the change in my temperament. "I don't know if I should really be seeing *anyone*," she says.

I wait for more, taking another sip.

"I'm not sure how to," she waves her hand in the air at a loss for words. "I'm still-" She can't put a sentence together.

"I want to fuck you, Jules. Give me one good reason why there's a problem with that." I hold her gaze listing all the reasons in my head, but ignoring every last one of them. She needs someone to fuck, to hold her, someone to make her smile. I can do that; I can be that person.

"It's just sex?" she asks me.

Fuck, I wish it were. I can't explain why I want her this badly. It's more than physical attraction, but I'll never admit the truth to her.

"Just sex," I lie.

She licks her lush lips, looking down at her silverware and then up to me. "I'd be using you," she confesses as if it's a sin.

A bark of a laugh leaves me, and my tense muscles relax.

"Use me, Jules." I stare into her eyes, feeling the tension between us morph into something sweeter, something darker and depraved. "I want you to."

CHAPTER 14

Julia

It starts with a kiss,
Then dinners and dates.
It starts with a smile,
Your evenings running late.
It tempts and teases,
And makes you want more.
But it's not how it starts,
When it can only end in war.

THERE'S something about him tonight. Something darker that I didn't see before. It's the way he looks at me like I should be running from him. It both scares me and lures me in.

I lift the glass to my lips, my one and only glass, finishing off the sweet wine.

"Did you write today?" Mason asks. We've made a bit of small talk and easy conversation. But I'm still feeling him out. I thought I wanted this thing between us, but the air changed a bit ago and the tension is something else now. Like we're at war, although I don't know why.

"I did, yes." All morning I wrote. The words flowed so easily. Every bit of it was about Jace though, something I'd rather not bring up with Mason. I pick up my glass, finding it empty and cursing internally.

"So, poetry?" he asks with a teasing tone. I'm not sure why I like it. I'm not a fan of being teased, but there's something about the way he does it that makes me want more of it.

I nod my head and explain, "I haven't tried writing anything else." I shrug, spearing my fork through the perfectly grilled salmon and savoring the taste. "It's easier to just write poetry."

"I'm not so sure. Isn't it easier to critique in some ways?"

His response catches me off guard, as if he actually gives a fuck.

"In some ways, I would think so. Maybe." I tilt my head, searching his eyes for what's really going on here. "Why dinner tonight? And not drinks?"

My voice is low, nearly accusatory, but he doesn't seem to mind.

"Because I had to eat and so did you," he replies.

He takes another bite of his dinner and then adds, "Would you rather I'd just asked you out for drinks?"

"Yes," I say and my answer is immediate. He doesn't seem taken aback. He's so calm, unmoving and unbothered.

"Why's that?" he asks.

I can't look him in the eyes, so I watch my fingers nervously move up and down the silverware. I don't know how to put it out there. "How did you know my name?" I ask him.

"From the papers," Mason says and then quickly takes a sip of his drink.

I nod my head. That's how everyone knows me. "The papers?"

"I've read a few things," he adds.

"Then you may have me at a clear disadvantage." I relax in my chair, waiting for him to tell me something.

"That's possible, probable even." He smirks at me, his brilliant smile adding to his charm. I try not to let it affect me, but I'm at his mercy whenever he looks at me like that. I grab on to the facts and spit out a good reason I have to stay away.

I'm vulnerable. Check.

I've never done this before. Check.

I don't know that I'm okay with this. Check.

And a man like Mason could crush me. Check a thousand times.

"Well, all I know of you is that you're a bit of player," I tell him as I hold his gaze.

"I used to be, yes."

"Used to?" I look up at him through my lashes, daring him to lie. There's a tension steadily growing between us. It's hot to the touch and it makes me want to climb closer to him, but I know that I need to stay far away.

"I mean it. I used to be, then I met someone." Well, that's enough to cool me off some.

"Oh." I'm surprised by his confession, and suddenly I feel like I should be asking him if he's sleeping with anyone else.

"She's gone, and it wasn't anything serious at all." He answers my questions before I have to ask them, and I'm grateful for that. "It just changed things for me."

"So now you just want someone to fuck and to take to dinners."

A deep rough chuckle vibrates up his chest and the way he smiles at me does something to me that makes me feel dirty.

"Someone, no." His eyes heat and he licks his bottom lip as he adds, "You, yes."

I huff out a small breath and look down at my mostly eaten plate.

"I want to take you out, bring you back home and fuck you in my bed." He holds my eyes as he says the words so calmly. I fight the urge to look around the room filled with fine guests and couples to make sure no one's heard us. My body is on fire with the thought of him doing just that, over and over. But the taking me out part... that makes this seem serious.

"I feel ..." I don't know how I feel.

"What's wrong?" he asks.

"I don't really like going out anymore." I blurt out the words and feel sick to my stomach.

"You don't like going out?"

"It just makes me anxious because of something that happened, that maybe you read about."

He stares at me for a moment and remains silent, although his eyes flash with a knowing look.

I don't want to say it out loud and I wait for him to speak, but he doesn't.

"It's just," my voice gets tight and I choke on the words, but only for a moment, "my husband passed away and it's hard for me to deal with it all because we were..."

"In the papers?" he asks.

"Yes. It's hard seeing people and not being with him. That's difficult for me." It feels like a weight's been lifted off my chest just to say it. "I don't know how to handle people's expectations."

Mason's words come out hard, and it's a command if I've ever heard one. "Fuck their expectations."

I'm shocked by how blunt Mason is. I don't think he understands. "I just don't want to upset people or-"

"Fuck. Them."

I stare at him, thinking he can't be serious, but he is. His eyes hold an intensity that makes me shiver involuntarily, and his hard muscular arms are corded. He flexes his stubbled jaw and seems to relax slightly, but I'm still caught off guard. Mostly because I want to obey him. I want to eat up every word he's saying as if it's law and bow down to him.

"You're entitled to feel and do whatever you want. It's no one else's business. Their perception of you is their responsibility. Not yours."

I take in a breath, hating that he doesn't understand. "Maybe I'm just shallow." I didn't mean to say it out loud, but I did. My breath leaves me and I pick up the empty glass again. Before I have the chance to roll my eyes or slam it on the table out of frustration, the waiter comes to my rescue, the bottle of chardonnay in his hand.

"Thank you," I say gratefully.

The second the waiter leaves, taking both of our plates with him, Mason says, "We can play this however you'd like."

"I don't really want to go out yet. I'm just not ready."

"Is it because you loved him?" Mason asks. His forehead is wrinkled and his brow furrowed. He can't even look me in the eye.

"I loved my husband, but that's not why." I take a sip of wine and staring at the glass I answer, "I just don't know how to not feel guilty about being okay."

The words came out easier than I thought they would. It's comforting to talk to Mason. I don't know why, but it is.

"So you're alright?" Mason asks me and he's so genuine with his concern that I reach across the table and take his hand in mine, rubbing soothing circles over his knuckles.

"Some days are better than others, but it's hard because I wasn't much without him."

Mason takes my hand in his at my comment, squeezing my hand and opening his mouth to say something, but nothing comes out. I take in a heavy breath, realizing how deep our conversation has gotten.

"I'm sorry," I say shaking my head and pulling my hand away. "I didn't mean to-"

"Stop apologizing," he tells me in a tone that makes all of my worries vanish. "I asked you, remember?"

I nod my head and utter a small response although I don't remember how the conversation started.

"Tell me something that will make me smile," he says.

A grin plays on my lips at the thought of him smiling at me and I say, "You're a very handsome man. Very charming. Obviously successful." I lean in slightly, letting the tips of my fingers play along his large knuckles and add, "And I really, really liked last night."

I accomplish my task and sit back in my seat, staring at his handsome face.

"I'm glad you enjoyed it." He keeps his eyes on me as we both take sips of our drinks. "I would have liked to have had you this morning as well."

I almost choke on the bit of wine, but luckily I save myself, swallowing it and taking a moment to get myself together.

"About that…"

"I imagine you'll make up for it tomorrow morning," he says like it's a statement, but I hear the question.

Another night with Mason Thatcher.

"I did say I was just along for the ride," I say to both him and to myself.

CHAPTER 15

Mason

Pretend it didn't happen,
Don't let the truth show.
Curiosity will lead you,
Exactly where you should go.
She'll lure you and tempt you,
And bid you farewell.
It's only then you'll realize,
You've wound up in hell.

I COULD BLAME the first night we spent together on shock and alcohol. The second on sheer curiosity. But this shit, this deep need to watch her, to touch her, to have her? There's no fucking excuse for it.

I stare at the computer screen mindlessly. The office is empty, and even Liam's gone home, leaving me here alone with simple tasks that should have already been done.

I have to audit this inventory and compare the replacement materials. It's crucial for the budget that this works, and I need to make the decision today.

But I really just don't give a fuck. I want all this to stop so I can hit pause. Instead I'm falling down a black pit, forced to make a choice of what will happen when I crash at the bottom.

Every penny is accounted for and spent, except for this last purchase. All of it is for one massive project. And all of it I owe to my father.

I sit forward in my chair, hitting the mouse to my computer and it lights the screen up once again. Two gorgeous blue eyes stare back at me. Her long thick lashes frame them perfectly. Her skin is flawless with only a hint of color in her cheeks. But it's her expression that had me staring at her all morning. Her lips are parted as if she's about to smile. So close to happiness, but the photo caught her before she reached that point.

It's only been two days since I've seen her, but each night I've felt a compulsion to message her and make sure I knew right where she was. I really wanted to make sure she wasn't with someone else. That's the truth of the matter. I trust her when she says she's not fucking someone else, but I know what loneliness can do to a person. And I want her all to myself.

If I just pretend like none of the shit before I met Jules happened, then there isn't a damn thing wrong with what's going on. If only it were that easy to forget.

Knock. Knock.

My gaze lifts to the clock on the wall and then to the door to my office. It's past 8 p.m. and almost time to meet Jules.

"Who is it?" I ask, not knowing who the hell it could be. Maintenance, maybe?

"Your partner in crime," Liam says from the other side of the door, and I relax slightly.

"Come on in," I yell out to him, clicking on my phone and seeing a text from Jules. She's waiting for me. The very thought spreads a warmth through my chest.

I set the phone down, giving Liam my full attention although I have no idea why the fuck he's here.

"You seem preoccupied?" Although it's a statement, it comes out as a question. Before I can even think about it, Liam's eyes are on the computer screen.

It's an innocent glance, but he doesn't need to see her. More importantly, he doesn't need to know about my new obsession. I'm quick to exit out of the article of Jules. It was about her husband's passing and how she was dealing with the loss. Although the picture they used of her was from years before.

I've read dozens of articles in the last few days. They're all the same. Every single one of them ooh and aah over her. They put her on a pedestal and in such a delicate place that it's far too easy for her to crash and burn.

And in some cases she did. The one fucking image I can't get out of my head is the one of her crying at her husband's funeral. Maybe they showed mercy by using an older photo for that article, because on the day she buried him she looked as if she'd died herself.

I take in a deep breath, willing the memory to go away. Wishing I'd never seen it.

"Well now," Liam says, ignoring my irritation. "Is this-"

"What are you doing here?" I ask, cutting him off and leaning back in my chair with my shoulders squared. He's still standing and leaning against the desk casually, but my tone has that fucking smile vanishing instantly.

He rubs the back of his neck, raising his brow and looking beyond me and out of the window as he takes a step back. "I was just wondering if you'd put the final numbers in."

I clear my throat, feeling like an absolute prick. "Sorry, it's been a tense day." I roll my shoulders, stretching my sore muscles and click on the spreadsheet. "I was just getting ready to put them in."

"So it's all finalized?" Liam asks with a chipper smile, seeming to forget I'm a fucking prick just like that.

"So far, so good." I force a smile and try to shake off the unease flowing through me. I can't explain the dichotomy of how I think of Jules. I want to take her out, impress her and please her in every way, include showing her off and showing off for her. But I want it to be my secret. I don't want anyone close to me to have an idea of what's going on between us.

It's a design for failure. I can't fucking help what I want though.

He claps his hands once and says, "Perfect. That's all I wanted to know." He raises his hands in defense as he starts to walk away, but then he looks back at me. The curiosity in his eyes asks to pry.

"What?" I ask him, my heart beating loudly in my chest. I don't know if I should deny whatever question he has about Jules. Everything in me is screaming to deny it all. I can never let anyone know.

"So... Julia Summers?" the prick has the balls to ask me.

I let out a deep breath and nod my head once. I can't help that I feel a sense of pride as his cocky smile widens. He twists the wedding band around his finger and nods his head.

"Well now, I guess I can forgive you for being such an irritable fuck lately."

"Watch it," I say under my breath but the smile on my face only leads him on.

"Good for you," he says and looks back at the screen, but it's only a spreadsheet of boxes and numbers. "So is it serious?" he asks, and I don't know why. He's never asked me before about who I'm fucking or dating, for that matter.

He answers the unasked question. "You just seem very preoc-cupied recently."

I move my seat closer to the desk, stretching my back and then shrugging, doing my best to appear casual. "Just a lot on my mind," I say.

He waits for a moment, expecting more, but I return to the spreadsheet. "I'll have it done before I leave," I tell him, giving him a tight smile and ending the conversation.

He leaves quietly, merely waving a goodbye and letting the door shut with a loud click, filling the empty room on his way out.

I look up when it's closed and tap the pen against the desk. I don't know what to deny, what to keep secret. I can't confuse the two, but the lines are already blurred.

CHAPTER 16

Julia

THIS IS NOT A DATE.
This is not serious.
This isn't something that needs to be more.
This is for fun.
This is pretend...

My pen stops on the last line. I stare at the words I've scribbled into the notepad, but my mind is blank. I don't know what I intended for this poem to be. Inspirational maybe?

But instead it all just looks like lies to me.

I click the end of my pen over and over. Click. Click. Click. Click. I'm debating on ripping this sheet out of the notebook and leaving it here.

The clink of several ceramic mugs being placed on top of one another behind me makes me turn to look over my shoulder. I inhale the rich smell of coffee in the small shop. The floors are checkered and the walls plain white, but this place serves the best coffee downtown. It's also right across from Mason's office, and I told him I'd meet him here. My eyes drift up, my thumb still on the end of my pen.

The Rising Falls Building is sleek and modern. It looks like a polished black obelisk all the way up, with a thick steel frame that's a matte black separating the glass panels. It's tall and dominating, ruling over the small buildings across from it.

It's everything Mason is.

I shouldn't be here, jotting down lies in a notepad and waiting for him. I pick up my coffee and take a sip. It's not hot anymore, but it's not room temperature either. The Styrofoam container feels just right in my hand as I take in a deep breath.

I keep telling myself I shouldn't be with him. I don't do casual, and this definitely doesn't seem casual but so far it's been several days of casual hooking up. But since when does waiting for your date mean it's casual?

Maybe I'm looking into things too much. It's only been a week and a half. It's just sex... or so I keep telling myself. *Maybe I should add that to the list of lies in my notepad.* I snort at the snide thought.

We aren't seeing each other in public, mostly. Not for events, anyway. It's not like anyone will notice or think anything of this. Even if they did, who cares?

There are whispers that I'm dating, but nothing that seems malicious or judgmental. Which is better than I'd hoped.

My heart beats hard in my chest at the thought, and the small air of confidence leaves me. I would care if they said I was a bitch for moving on too soon. Or that I'm no longer the good girl. That Jace's death was in some ways my death, too. They wouldn't be wrong about that one.

I don't want Jace's father seeing that I've moved on. Or my mother. I close my eyes and try to rid myself of the image of her seeing a snapshot of the other night in a paper with her morning tea. Drunk at a bar with a strange man holding me. I groan, rubbing my temples. Yeah, I don't need my mother seeing that.

The bells hanging above the front door jingle, and my eyes instinctively open.

There he is, Mason, taking the breath in my lungs as he strides toward me. I'm stuck as I sit there, pinned to my seat watching the air of confidence he gives off. His steel grey eyes look darker than ever as he grabs the back of the chair across from me and pulls it out. The legs scrape on the floor, protesting him sitting with me, but he claims it and fixes those eyes on me.

"Jules," he says and my name falls from his gorgeous lips in a rough baritone and I finally breathe.

"Mason," I say his name and then smile, I don't know why. I just can't help it. He makes me feel... like a little girl caught in a fantasy. It's the way he wears his suit, the way he walks into buildings, the way he looks at me. As if he owns them all.

A small smile plays on his lips as well. I did that. I made him smile.

He gestures toward my cup and asks, "Should I get one as well?"

I sit up straighter and look over my shoulder again at the counter with the one lonely register and stacks and stacks of mugs behind it. It's late, but this coffee shop never closes, because this city never sleeps.

"If you'd like to," I answer and then turn to face him. He reaches across the table, and tucks a strand of hair behind my ear. His eyes and hands linger on the exposed part of my neck. The tips of his fingers trail down my neck slowly, with purpose. I feel the heat race through me, the desire creeping slowly from where our skin touches down my chest, and lower... and lower. He confuses me when I'm near him. I can't think of anything but what I want him to do to me, and that's a dangerous thing.

I want to close my eyes, but I can't. I'm mesmerized by the way he looks at me. The steel grey gaze seems softer, and the harsh lines of his jaw seem less intimidating, more vulnerable.

"I think if I do," he finally answers, leaning back to retake his seat, "I'd like to get it to go."

I nod my head vigorously and then feel foolish as he lets out a rough laugh. The bells jingle in the doorway just as he leans across the table for a kiss.

Anxiety shoots through me, and I pull back as soon as his scorching hot lips touch mine. My back hits the hard plastic of the chair and my eyes whip over to an old man in a tweed suit. His white hair looks ruffled from the wind, but he doesn't care. His light blue eyes gaze through his thick rimmed glasses over the counter and up at the menu behind me.

I look back at Mason, feeling slightly relieved that it wasn't anyone who would recognize us, but that doesn't last long. My heart drops when I see the look on his face.

I don't like to disappoint, but this is also something else. I feel guilty for pretending this is something it's not. But I have no fucking clue what this is, and I'm petrified to find out.

"I don't know..." I clear my throat trying to catch my breath, and give him the honest truth without being offensive. "I don't-"

"If you're with me," he says and the tone Mason gives me is authoritative. His eyes pierce into me, pinning me to my seat and stealing my excuses from the tip of my tongue. "Then you're *with me*." He finishes his thought and I can't look away, I can't breathe, I can't do anything but hold his gaze.

He finally breaks the hold he has on me, rising from his seat and buttoning his suit jacket. He doesn't look at me as he walks past me and up to the counter. I stare at the door, wondering if I should just leave. My body feels hot and I don't think I can do this. I still don't even know what *this* is.

It's definitely not "just sex."

My body stands on its own. Although my legs feel wobbly, my body weak and my head clouded with frustration and confusion, something inside me pushes me forward. It's only four steps, four strides toward him, and all the while my heart beats faster and my body heats.

"I don't know what *this* is," I start to say. My voice comes out strong, clear and full of a confidence I don't possess. "And that doesn't matter." I take in a breath as he cocks a brow at me and turns to face me fully. He gives me his full attention and waits for me.

A shaky breath comes and goes as I try to come up with the right words. "I don't know what I want." The words are so true. "I am not *with* anyone. I'm alone, and that's-" I cut myself off before I almost say that's how I want it. I almost lie to both him and myself.

I turn to my right as the barista looks away casually, as if she wasn't listening. My cheeks flame with embarrassment.

"If you want me to leave you alone, it's done."

I shake my head, my heart racing with fear. I resist the urge to reach out to him, feeling so fucking weak. "I want you," I whisper, my eyes pleading with his. "I just don't," I swallow and force my eyes to meet his. "I don't want people to know."

Fuck, I feel like an asshole. "I'm not ashamed of you... I'm just ashamed of me..." Oh God, even I cringe at my words. It's the truth, but it's so shitty of me. I swallow thickly, searching Mason's face for understanding or anger. But instead there's a coldness that greets me, and it fucking hurts. "I don't mean it to come out in a way that's offensive."

"It's because of your husband?" he finally asks me and I don't waste a second to answer, "Yes." The word is barely a breath.

"I want to take you home," he says and licks his lips and instinctively my eyes are drawn toward them. He lets his eyes roam down my body. "We can talk about this in bed."

My lips part, and I struggle not to look back at the barista who's no doubt watching us.

"Do you want that, Jules?" Mason asks me.

I do. I want him to touch me and hold me and make me feel alive.

Why is this so hard? It's my emotions, that's why. The poetry of life. Drawing me in and then snapping me out of it.

"Jules?" he asks, pushing me and I cave to what I really want. Because if I deny it, if I deny him, I may lose it forever.

I nod once, and he places his hand on the small of my back, leading me away from the counter and toward my jacket and coffee I've left on the table.

As I put the jacket on, trying to just calm the fuck down and stop making such a big deal out of nothing, Mason leans forward and whispers in the crook of my neck. "I don't know what I want, other than I want you... in my bed... every night." My pussy clenches and heats as his words register. A small wave of relief and arousal flood through my system. He lifts the jacket over my shoulders, helping me to put it in place and then looks me in the eyes.

"Is that something you want?" he asks.

That's what I want, but this seems like more.

I don't know how to separate the two. A relationship versus just someone to fuck.

It's going to be a problem for me, I already know it is, but telling Mason that in this moment is something I can't do. If I do, I've lost him.

Silence hovers between us for a moment, feeling hot and as if it slows the ticks of the clock in the room, time stalling and my mind whirling with how this is all going to end.

He's going to crush me. He'll leave me shattered when he's done.

He's not the first though, and there's not much of me that can break any more than I already have.

I put a small smile on my face and nod, feeling as though I'm being granted a death wish. "Yes," I tell him, holding his grey eyes, "I want that, too."

He doesn't know the truth, and I'm too much of a coward to tell him.

I've sealed my own fate in this moment. I know I have.

If only I hadn't said it. If only I could walk away.

CHAPTER 17

Mason

What's right and what's wrong are overrated,
The lines are blurred; consequences negated.
I'm left without truth, only the lies that I've built.
I'm left all alone, consumed by the guilt.

SHE'S NERVOUS AND ANXIOUS, quiet too. My car is the last one on this level in the garage. We walk in unison, my hand still on the small of her back. I'm not letting go until I have her in my car. She's on the verge of running, and I won't fucking allow it.

She needs to know that she belongs to me. She wants to hide this, and that's just fucking fine with me. But only so that she knows not to be ashamed. I won't be denied. Fuck that.

I'll give her everything she desires, because I want to. I want to see her smile, to hear that laugh that drew me to her. I'll do everything I can to make it up to her.

And she'll give me all of her in return.

I start to open the passenger side door to my car, but then I stop, shutting it before she has a chance to slip in.

My dick is hard; my blood is hot. I take a glance at Jules and her wide eyes stare back at me. They're the same eyes I've been looking at all day. But there's no hint of a smile, only concern, and a hint of rejection mixed into the soft blues of her eyes.

There's a large cement post to the right of my car, right where the entrance is. It's square in shape and maybe three feet wide. If someone drove up, it would block us for the moment. Only a moment, but the odds of someone coming here this late at night are slim and fixing this shit right now is worth taking the risk.

I take off my jacket and lead her to the front of the car, where we'll be hidden from view. Although her steps are hesitant, she takes my lead, looking over her shoulder and no doubt wondering what the hell is going on.

"Mason?" I can hear the hesitation in her voice as her ass bumps against the car.

I grab her hips in my hands and shove her back, pinning her down and crashing my lips against hers. Her hands fly to my chest pushing me away at first, caught off guard by the sudden change of plans, and then travel up my neck ever so slowly. She gives into me, moving her hands to the back of my head, pulling me in for more.

That's a good girl. My good girl. The woman who needs me, and I fucking need to make it up to her.

I break the heated kiss, her panting chest touching mine over and over again as I look down at her. "Be good for me and be quiet."

She nods her head, her breath still coming in fast through her parted lips. I crush mine to hers again and she moans into my mouth but before she can deepen it, I fist her hair in my hands and pull her away, grabbing her hips and flipping her over so her breasts are pressed against the metal.

"Stick your ass out for me," I tell her in a rough voice as I palm my dick through my pants and take a peek around the pillar. There's no one in sight, and I fucking need her tight pussy cumming on my dick.

She whimpers as I pull her head back by her hair and kiss her neck. She rocks her hips, and her hot pussy brushes against my dick, teasing me.

I'm quick to unzip my pants and pull my thick cock out, stroking it and finally letting her go. She lets out a gasp, bracing herself and looking over her slender shoulder at me with those gorgeous blue eyes full of lust... and trust.

I pull her panties to the side and kiss her neck once more before shoving myself deep inside her tight cunt. This has to be quick, no time for playing.

Her back arches and her fingers scrape along the hood, but she doesn't scream out. Nothing but a small gasp escapes her mouth. Her pussy spasms and feels like fucking heaven as I hold in a groan and put my hand on the small of her back, pressing her down and keeping her in place.

Her eyes are closed tight, and her teeth are sunk into her bottom lip. I rock out slightly and push back in, forcing the sweetest sound from those beautiful lips. A moan of pleasure.

I grip her chin in my hand and force her to look at me; I want her to watch me. I want her eyes on mine as I take her just how she needs. Right where I fucking want her.

Her eyes slowly open as she lets out a breath, and that's when I slam into her again. She bucks forward, a small cry uttering from her lips and I wait again for her to look back at me.

"You need to watch me, sweetheart," I tell her with an even voice even though my heart's pounding in my chest.

I'll show her who she belongs to and how fucking good I'll be to her. But she has to watch me, she needs to see it all and know this is exactly what she wanted. *That she wanted me.*

She rests her cheek against the car and keeps her eyes on me and I thrust into her again and again, pulling all the way out and slamming all the way back into sweet pussy.

The sound of tires above us makes her squirm beneath me, but they can't come down this way. I know because I park here every fucking day. I lean closer to her, pushing my chest against her back and kissing her gently on the lips. "They won't see." My hand slips between us and lifts the front of her dress up, teasing along her clit through the thin layer of fabric. I play with her, teasing and rubbing while watching her writhe under me. "Look at me," I command her and she's quick to turn her eyes to me. They seemed tortured with pleasure and the need to cry out her releases. She's fucking gorgeous and I could make this easy for her, I really could. I could fuck her quickly and take her over the edge so she doesn't have to fight the urge for long. I could let her close her eyes and look away.

But I'm not interested in that.

Jules is going to see. I won't let her think this is all pretend and something that it's not.

I'm going to give her everything she needs. I'm going to make it alright again, and she's going to love me for it. If that makes me a prick, I don't give a fuck.

I don't care how it's going to end, just that it happens this way. Right here, and right now.

"Mason," she whispers my name as her release takes her gently, her pussy squeezing my dick and sucking me deeper into her. Trying to milk me. But I'm not done with her yet. I wait for her to stop trembling before moving my fingers to my lips. They're slick with her arousal and taste like honey. I move my fingers down her throat and to the fabric of her dress. I wish she were naked so I could see every inch of her. So I could see the flush that's creeping up her chest.

"This is going to be quick," I tell her and then grab her hips in both my hands and angle her how I want her. I glance up to make sure she's still watching and just like the good girl she is, those doe eyes are on me. I piston my hips, surprising her as she braces her limp body against the car. The intensity of the raw fuck makes her gorgeous lips form a perfect "O" as her body tightens and her silent scream makes her head thrash. I fist her hair again and pull her back.

"Mason," she moans and my name is a twisted word of desperation on her lips.

"Cum for me," I tell her, moving my other hand to her clit again. The fabric of her dress clings to me as I push her panties down enough to strum her swollen nub.

She screams out for the first time, and I'm quick to bite her neck. Hard. It's a punishment for not obeying me, and it only makes her struggle against me harder. And only makes her pending orgasm that much more intense.

I fucking love it. I love what I do to her and how much pleasure it gives her.

Her body goes rigid, and her pussy tightens around my cock. She struggles to breathe and her head lolls back as she looks at the cement ceiling, her climax threatening to crash through her.

I nip her chin and move the hand that was gripping her hair to her face. I stare into her eyes as her body shudders and her neck arches, her hair draping over my shoulder. Her face is the epitome of sinful ecstasy. It's the most beautiful thing I've ever seen.

"Fuck," I groan as she finds her release. Her tight cunt strangles my cock; she feels like fucking heaven. It only takes four more pumps, riding through her orgasm and taking her that much higher until I find my own release. My balls draw up, and my spine tingles. Fuck, yes. I bury my head in her neck as my cock pulses deep inside of her cunt.

The sounds of our heavy breathing surround us for a long moment.

I kiss the side of her neck right where the faint red marks are from my bite, running my nose along her soft skin and breathing in her scent as she breathes heavily against the car. Her legs are still trembling and a shudder runs down her body as I pull my lips away from her. She's perfectly sated, just as she should be.

"You're mine, Jules," I tell her in a whisper that's loud enough for her to hear and watch for her reaction. Her long lashes flutter as she opens her eyes and looks back at me. I pull her panties back into place and fix her dress, knowing damn well my cum will be leaking out of her the second she sits down in the car.

"Mason," she whimpers my name, and her forehead creases as her eyes beg with me to take it back.

"No, you want me and I want you."

She bites down on her bottom lip and says, "I'm not okay." Her voice hitches, and her words crack. She closes her eyes and speaks as if it truly pains her to say the words. "I don't know if I can be good for you." Her large eyes look back at me as she adds, "I'm broken."

I rest my forehead against hers and ask, "Why are you so afraid?"

"I don't think this can just be sex for me," she admits. I cup her jaw in my hand and brush my thumb across her cheek. "I think I'm going to want more. I think I already-" she cuts herself off and shakes her head.

My body feels tense, each breath hurting my chest. Why am I doing this to her? Why can't I just let her go? "I can give you more," I whisper in the air between us, knowing it's what she wants to hear. "We can just see how it works between us, and be quiet in public?"

I'm giving her exactly what she wants, just to keep her.

I'm a prick for doing it, knowing it can never be what she really needs and wants.

But her eyes light up, and that soft smile comes back to me. She brightens with hope, and my shy girl comes back to me.

"Really?" she asks, still panting, barely recovered from what I've already done to her.

She has no idea that she should be running from me. And I'm well aware I should turn her away regardless. Instead I smile down at her and kiss the tip of her nose. "Really," I answer and hate myself that much more.

CHAPTER 18

Julia

There's nothing wrong with mourning,
But know it doesn't easily pass.
The tears and heartbreak are still coming,
This moment of pain surely won't be the last.
There's no reason to be ashamed,
What you once had long ago was love.
The memories won't ever fade,
They'll come as they please.

THERE'S no rhyme or reason for when the memories come back. There's nothing I can see that causes it. There's nothing I can blame.

Lying in Mason's arms, naked and warm, the two of us each

working on our laptops in comfortable silence. There's not a damn reason that I should be thinking of Jace, but I am.

I didn't want to. I scoot my back close to the sofa and try to get the images of him smiling at me out of my head. When I'd wake up in the morning, Jace would push the hair from my face and give me a quick kiss. Always on the lips, no matter how much I tried to dodge it. He thought it was cute how I didn't want him to smell my morning breath.

Moments like that, moments we shared together that were easy and fun, where we fit beautifully together, those hurt the most. I let out an uneasy sigh and try to calm down, ignoring Mason's eyes on me.

You'd think I'd be happy I had that at one point in time. That I had a man who loved me and who I loved, too. It's easy to say I'll be glad because it happened and not sad because it's over. But the truth is I can't say that. I can't say it and mean it.

"What's wrong?" Mason's deep voice makes me feel even worse. I'm trying to just move on, but it's not that easy.

I swallow the lump in my throat and pull the dark grey throw over my legs and up to my shoulders. "Just having a moment," I tell him honestly, although I can't look him in the eyes. I hope he'll just let it go.

I hear his heavy breath as he pulls me closer to him and kisses my hair. I don't expect the gentle touch from him. He whispers, "I get it."

He splays his hand on my hip and runs his thumb back and forth over my bare skin. I wait for more, but he doesn't say anything.

My laptop jostles across my legs as I try to get closer to him, loving the warmth, needing more of it. This is so wrong, isn't it? To be upset over the passing of your husband while you're in the arms of your lover.

"Sometimes-" Mason starts to speak just as my eyes glaze over and the words on the screen start to blur. I take in a steadying breath and stop that shit. Crying never helped me. It doesn't do any good.

Mason clears his throat while I wipe under my eyes, my cheeks flaming from embarrassment and my heart racing like crazy.

"When my mom died, sometimes it was the oddest things that set me off." I'm surprised by Mason's confession, and grateful to be talking about him and not me.

"I'm sorry about your mom," I tell him softly, my voice a bit scratchier than I'd like. I stare up into his eyes, and they're so much lighter than usual, maybe because it's dark all around us. Only the glow of the laptops and the city lights beyond the large living room window to paint the room in a soft glow.

He tilts his head to the side, tucking my hair behind my ear and I push my cheek into his palm. He has such large hands, rough but warm. And the perfect size for this.

A coarse hum comes from deep in his chest. It's short, but a sound of approval.

"It's okay to hurt still," he tells me. "It's okay to cry and let it out, even if you're already spent."

My heart beats harder, my breathing becoming more difficult. I search his eyes for something, and he must see the panic in mine.

"Or we can do something else?" he offers.

"Like what?" I ask him.

He clucks his tongue, his gaze on my face, but not my eyes. Finally, he takes his hand away, and types something into the search bar on his computer.

A surprised gasp slips through my lips as he pulls up a book of poetry. Robert Frost.

I eye him curiously and he pets my hair before pulling my head in to rest on his shoulder. I get comfortable as he says, "I can read to you?"

My heart hurts so much in this moment. Not the pain of what I've lost, but the pain that I have something so beautiful and something I'm so grateful for, and yet I still have these moments.

I nod into his shoulder and whisper, "Please."

I could listen to his deep, rugged voice read poetry to me in the dark for hours.

I could rest in his warm embrace for days.

I could stay here with this man forever.

CHAPTER 19

Mason

When it's too good to be true, deep down you know.
You don't want to hold on, because it's certain to go.
But you get lost in the moment, the desire and trust
'cause when it's this good to you, you know it's not lust.

IT WASN'T SUPPOSED to be like this. It wasn't supposed to be this much more. I watch Jules as she licks the ice cream from her spoon, her tongue flat against the bottom and mindlessly watches the news.

Her notepad is in her lap, the pen on top. She was writing when I walked in here. It's 4 a.m., and she can't sleep.

My mother used to feed me ice cream every night before bed. I had to be in my room and under the sheets as soon as I was finished, but I got ice cream every night. All sorts of flavors, because I was never picky. Mom always ate strawberry though; it was her favorite.

Jules glances over at me, a flirtatious look in her eyes. "Do you want some?" she asks me, maneuvering her body in catlike motions to crawl over to me.

I shake my head no, but I can feel a small smile on my lips as I wrap my arm around her and place my hand on her thigh to scoot her closer to me.

She moans softly as she scoops up half of the last bit of cherry ice cream in the bowl. That shit has to be intentional, but she's still watching the television as if it's not. I pick my ass up slightly off the couch and readjust myself in my pajama pants.

She peeks at me, blushing and brushes her arm against my bare chest.

"You're sweet to get me this," she says with that look in her eyes. The look that tells me I've made her happier than she thought I would. "Thank you," she adds and plants a small kiss on my shoulder.

I didn't mind. Truthfully, I couldn't sleep either. I felt her leave, the absence of her warmth the moment she left the bed. For such a graceful woman, she's not very quiet getting out of bed.

I gave her a few minutes to see what she would do. I peeked in the doorway as she got lost in her words. Watching as she sat cross-legged on the sofa, leaning over and scribbling like mad. It wasn't until she started to cry that I came into the room. I thought she needed me. I thought it was about him.

But she said they were happy tears, like closure. I don't know why that hurts me more.

"No problem, I wanted to get out anyway."

"Did you go for a run?" she asks me, eating the last of the ice cream and facing me. I shake my head no. I don't have time for that right now. Usually she's in bed when I run and then shower.

"It's my fault?" she asks and scrunches her nose, not liking that she's thrown off my routine.

"It doesn't matter," I tell her. And it truly doesn't. "I'll make it up later tonight."

She hums a small sound and then adjusts on the sofa.

She straddles me on the sofa, a leg on either side of mine until she settles into my lap. I let my hands rest on her ass cheeks as she drops the empty bowl and spoon beside us on the sofa, the spoon clinking as she shoves them further away.

"Mr. Thatcher," she says as she wraps her arms around my neck and squares her shoulders, "I do believe you're going to be late today."

I smirk at her, looking at the clock behind her first to be sure she's lost her damn mind, and she has. I have at least another hour before I need to get going. "I think you may be mistaken, sweetheart," I tell her.

She rocks her hot pussy against me and gives me a smoldering look. It's one I don't get often, one full of confidence and determination. But fuck, when she does give it to me, it drives me wild.

"You need your exercise, Mr. Thatcher." She drops her voice low and slides the straps to her silk nightgown down, exposing her plump breasts. They're small, but fit perfectly in my hand.

My dick stirs in my pants and I sit farther back on the sofa, rocking my hips and making her gasp as she reaches out to steady herself by clinging to me.

My hands wrap around her small waist as she kisses my jaw. I don't know when it happened, but my control has waned with Jules. And I fucking love it.

This is such a fucking mess. A beautiful mess.

CHAPTER 20

Julia

Happy is relative,
An emotion in time.
Guilt waits in shadows,
Makes you pay for your crime.
When push comes to shove,
And the two have to meet.
You'll be judged, never loved,
It's all bittersweet.

I BREATHE in the smell of the hot coffee in my hands. It's the best damn smell this early in the morning. That, or the smell of Mason's pillow. I don't know what it is about the way he smells that drives me crazy. Each morning I pull his pillow out from under him and take it as his alarm goes off.

I can't stop the smile that spreads across my face remembering this morning how he flipped me over and "punished" me for it. This feels like more and it seems too fast, but for the first time in a long damn time, I'm happy. Genuinely happy.

"Stop smiling like that," Maddie says across the table as she blows on her latte. She lifts the white cup to her lips and eyes me before taking a sip. The smile doesn't fade; her comment only makes it grow larger. "You're making me jealous."

"That is the power of sex," Sue says as she takes a seat, a Styrofoam cup in her hand so I imagine she'll be leaving shortly. She sets her bag on the floor and slips onto the stool easily. "It's about time you girls caught on and started getting some." A coy smile lifts the corners of her lips up as she adds, "Well, except Kat since she's married."

Maddie laughs into her cup and Kat gives Sue a cold look for a moment and then shrugs. "He's good at what he does," Kat says, but we all know there have been some complaints recently in the bedroom.

Whenever Kat looks at me, it takes me down from this high. She represents what I once had and what I should really be striving for. She has a loving husband, a stable and growing career, and shit, she's my boss really. Children are definitely in her future.

I set my cup down on the table and try to stop being... jealous. Is it jealousy? How can it be when I am enjoying getting lost in Mason's touch?

I'm being reckless. That's what it really comes down to. For the first time in my life, I don't have a set plan, and I'm being fucking stupid.

"Is it weird?" Maddie asks me as she crumples Kat's straw wrapper on the table. She has both hands on it, balling up the small white paper into a perfect sphere. "Like since you were only with Jace?" she adds, and then peers up at me, gauging my reaction.

The mention of his name... fuck. It still affects me. I think it always will.

"Yeah, kinda. At first." I take a sip of coffee and hate that there's a comparison at all. "I feel like it's cheating on him," I croak out, my chest feeling tight.

"Um no, that's what he did to you," Sue says with a firm voice that grabs my attention. She rests a hand on my forearm. "Moving on is *not* cheating." She purses her lips with her eyes on me as if she doesn't know whether or not she should say what's on her mind.

"Say it." My voice is strong. I just want to get it out there, like pulling off a Band-Aid. Even if it hurts, I need to hear it.

"I worry about you and Mason. It doesn't have a damn thing to do with Jace." She waves her hand through the air as she shakes her head once and then continues. "You know I never liked him much, especially after hurting you." *Cheating.* After cheating on me. That's what she means. We'd only ever been with each other. His explanation was that he was curious, and it was a mistake. And so I forgave him. We moved past that together. Sue never did but it wasn't her marriage, and it wasn't her decision.

"Why are you worried?" I ask her, running my nails along the edge of the cup and removing the thoughts of that infidelity from my mind. "It's nothing serious." I bite the inside of my cheek; even to me that sounded like a fucking lie.

"That right there," Sue leans back and points her finger at me. "I worry that you don't know what casual dating is or a fuck-buddy, or whatever this is for Mason."

I struggle with the confession, but I have to be honest with them. They may have their opinions and stick their noses where they don't belong, but they always have my best interests at heart. I clear my throat and spit it out. "He said he could give me more."

"What?" Maddie pipes up, scooting her stool closer to the table. Her pink cardigan is pulled down tight across her dress as she leans forward and asks, "What did he mean by 'more'?"

"Yeah, what the fuck did he mean by 'more'?" Sue asks, skepticism obvious. Even Kat's looked up from her phone to listen.

"I don't know. I just..." I pause and look back at Sue. "I was worried too and I told him that I didn't know if I could handle it because I would probably want more, and he said he could give me that." I think back to that night, just two nights ago and I'm fairly certain that's exactly what happened. It makes me feel secure, that I can be open about how I'm feeling and that he's receptive to it. It makes me feel... cherished in a way. Respected at least.

Maddie lets out a small sigh of satisfaction, like a young girl in puppy love; she's obviously the only one happy about what I've said. Sue taps her nails rhythmically on the table and Kat hasn't moved, still watching me like a hawk watches its prey in the sky. Circling, waiting to strike.

Jesus, and these are my friends. I steady myself and take a sip of coffee.

"I just don't understand why?" Kat says, setting her phone down and turning her attention to me. "Why him?"

Mason is nothing like the man I *should* be with. But that man is gone, and I'm not interested in replacing him.

"It's just for fun," I answer her. Lies. God, it's such a lie!

"But it's not. You just said it's not. So I don't get it." For once in my life, I wish Kat wouldn't call me out on my bullshit. I wish they'd all just turn a blind eye to the obvious downfall I'm headed toward. Just like I'm doing.

I take another drink of coffee, feeling defensive and like I'm not sure that I really want to even have this conversation.

"You're not going to settle down with him," Kat says and waits for me to look at her before continuing, "right?"

"I'm not settling down or replacing-" Jace's name gets caught in my throat.

"I feel like you may be setting yourself up for a major breakup." Kat holds my gaze and I fucking hate that she says it, because I feel the same. But it's so good right now. And I just want to live in this moment, because this moment feels so damn right. Well it did before my friends chimed in.

"Maybe he's a rebound," Sue says with a shrug and then looks up at the menu on the other side of the room. The whiteboard travels from wall to wall and the text is fairly large, but she's not reading it. All four of us have that menu memorized.

"Yeah," I agree with her, holding up my cup of coffee and looking back at Kat for what her response will be to that.

"I'm just worried," Kat says softly and picks her phone back up, but she doesn't look at it. She bites down on her lip as she asks, "Can we meet him?"

"For fuck's sake, Kat," Sue says from across the table, practically glaring at her. "You don't introduce a rebound to your friends."

"Is that a rule?" Kat bites back.

"It's weird!" Sue's brow is comically raised as she stares back at Kat like she can't be serious.

"I'd like to meet him," Maddie says with a sweet innocent tone that doesn't match the other two.

"I think no," I answer all three of them at once. "It's just sex, but there's a level of respect and understanding." I nod my head once. "That's what the *more* is."

I take in a deep breath, feeling like I've fixed my nonexistent problem. That's exactly what this is. It's just a mutually beneficial arrangement with respect... and sex, of course.

Both Kat and Sue are silent, each nodding and probably unhappy with the decision, each for their own reason, but I don't care.

"I have a meeting with my CPA," I tell them as I glance down at my phone. I was going to walk there, but there's no way in hell I'm going to make it now. "I gotta go," I huff out as I reach down to grab my Marc Jacobs tote off the floor.

"Hey," Kat says, giving me her full attention. "Are you happy?" she asks me with all seriousness.

I stand up, slinging the purse over my shoulder and pushing the stool back. Licking my lips, I nod my head.

"Yeah," I tell her and that smile comes back. "I'm happy."

I expect some kind of guilt or feeling of inevitable doom, but all the girls smile and Maddie squeals with delight. My chest feels empty, as if I'm lying to myself and afraid that someone will expose my lie. But I am happy. This is what happiness feels like, isn't it?

"That's what matters," Kat says with finality.

"Damn right," Sue adds her two cents, grabbing her purse to join me.

"Wanna share a cab?" she asks, the conversation of Mason and whatever the hell I'm doing with him long gone. At least for now.

CHAPTER 21

Julia

Time keeps moving, even if you stand still.
Grief keeps you down, all against your will.
It's not to be overcome, it's not left in the past.
This pain in my heart, this pain is meant to last.

I HATE BEING HERE in this office. It's always so dark. I don't understand why Mr. Allen Walker doesn't open a damn curtain. The plain white shades aren't thick, but they're very good at blocking out what little sunlight would shine through the windows to my right. The office practically butts up against the building next door. Through the small gap where the fabric should meet, I can see the old brick from Parks Towers next door. I'd rather look at that and have some damn sunlight than the curtains.

I scoot back on the chair, my purse in my lap feeling more and more uncomfortable.

"Miss Summers," Allen addresses me as he always has, since I was a little girl and after I was married, but it feels different now. He shuts the door behind him, a smile on his face as he shoves the thin-rimmed glasses up the bridge of his nose. Fine lines and wrinkles crease around his eyes as he holds out a hand for me. I stand up, the lightweight chair sliding back on the thin carpet as I shake his hand.

"It's been too long," he says warmly. I nod my head and smile politely, although I disagree.

The last time I was here was a few days after Jace passed away. That day, Allen made sure to call me by my legal name and not the name I grew up with. The memory makes the tiny hairs on the back of my neck stand on edge as I clear the lump in my throat and retake my seat. Uncomfortable as it may be, it's the only one I've got.

It seems he's forgotten that Summers still isn't my legal name. I look down at my barren hand and think that's my fault. I took my wedding ring off months ago. That was easy, all things considered, but changing my name is something else entirely. It's like erasing Jace, and I won't do that.

"It has," I say lightheartedly, pulling my light grey pencil skirt down and retaking my seat as he takes his on the other side of the desk.

My chair is small and uncomfortable, while his is large and practically molds to his body.

I shake out the anxiety running through me as I straighten my back and ask, "What is it that you needed me to sign?"

A rough laugh fills the room as he shakes his head. "No, nothing to sign. I need decisions, Miss Summers."

My body tenses at my name, but I bite my tongue. "Of course, and what decisions?"

"As acting advisor to your estate and investments, I need you to look these over," he says as he pulls out several folders and sets them in front of me. My brow pinches as I open the first and then the second. It's shit I don't know a thing about. I've never been involved with these things, these investments and stocks.

"I," I start to say and let out an uneasy breath. "Is there a way that I could take your advisement, Mr. Walker?"

He turns his head to the side and raises his brow as if to say I should have done that a long time ago. "I advised your husband when he made these and unfortunately the choices now are to stay and keep your money in a losing bet, or to withdraw and lose a substantial amount."

My body goes cold as I take in his words. "I don't understand."

"Mr. Anderson was adamant about buying these properties and he assured me that it would be worth the risk, but I've waited over nine months now and still there's been no growth since the drop."

"The drop?" I ask him, feeling the blood drain from my face.

"It was on the decline when he purchased. He was a bit surprised that it continued to drop, yes." Mr. Walker leans back, waiting for my reaction.

"How much of a decline?"

"Fourteen million."

Holy fuck. I close my eyes, gripping onto the edge of the seat.

"There's still nearly six million invested, so you can withdraw if you'd like. I do like to say you've never lost money until you sell, but the fact is that I still believe you're not going to see the return your former husband was banking on."

My entire body is tense and on edge. Fourteen fucking million dollars. Fourteen million! I want to scream and curse, I want to throw the fuck up. It takes me a moment to gather myself to be able to respond.

"Why am I just learning about this now?" I ask him in a voice that's more filled with anger than with shock and grief. I flip over a few pages, leafing through them, but not actually reading a word.

Fourteen million. I'm going to be sick.

"Well it was stable, but it's recently gone up just a touch and I feel like you should take advantage of the current climate."

My mouth hangs open just a bit as I look back at Mr. Walker, eyeing his blue suit and thin red tie. I blink a few times, then fall back into my chair and shut the folder.

"Is this all of the investments?" I ask him. For the first time in my life, I'm worried. I've never had to concern myself with income. I've been blessed and grateful, but I sure as fuck wasn't careless. This right here, this feels like careless to the maximum degree and I'm embarrassed. I'm sick to my stomach and mortified.

I swallow thickly and cross my legs, not able to stop my foot from rocking back and forth in the air.

Fourteen million is quite a sum. It's not the most in the world or everything I have, and I know I'll always have my house, but it's enough that I know it's got to hurt.

It's only as I sit here, my mouth feeling dry and my body like ice, that I realize I know nothing about my current financial situation. I trusted Jace to handle all that.

"Allen," I say and pick at the clutch in my lap and look up at the man I grew up with. He's an old friend of my father's and I do trust him, but right now I feel unsettled.

"Yes, Julia?" he asks.

"Financially speaking," I pause, taking in a steadying breath, "is everything alright?"

He takes a moment to answer me and the time ticks by slowly, making my heart beat faster and my blood heat.

He opens his mouth, looking down at the desk but doesn't say a word and dread hits me. "You're going to be fine, Miss Summers. You will be," he puts strength behind his words and looks straight into my eyes as he replies.

Thank fuck, I'm almost bowled over by the intense relief.

"It's going to be difficult getting this money back, especially considering the amount of debt you went into remodeling your home."

"What?" I feel struck by his last statement. "We didn't go into debt." I got everything I wanted on that remodel because it was the money I'd made with my first publishing contract. It was my personal reward to myself. "I accounted for every penny, and I know it was paid for with the money I brought in."

I can't help that my voice is full of panic and my tone is accusatory. I sit there on the edge of my seat, waiting for a response from Allen. I swallow the lump in my throat as he clicks on his mouse and takes off his glasses, scrolling through a row of spreadsheets.

"The remodel put you in quite a bit of debt, I'm sorry to say."

I shake my head in disbelief as he adds, "If you were to sell the apartment, it could potentially make its money back." A chill travels down every inch of my body as I take one breath, then two. "What apartment?" I ask him, my voice deathly low.

"The one downtown on Pacific Street. The one that was remodeled."

My world spins on its axis, and I grip the arms of the chair. "Mr. Walker. I don't own an apartment." I lick my dry lips, my body coiled, my muscles feeling tense and tight.

"Well your husband did, and that was left to you as was everything else in his will."

"Why wasn't I told about this sooner?" I ask, focusing my attention on something other than the fact that my husband bought and remodeled an apartment without me knowing. Betrayal consumes me, but oddly I feel numb to it. As if I'd known all along. As if I'd turned a blind eye. 'Cause I'm fucking stupid. It's not naiveté or my trusting nature. It's me being fucking stupid and gullible. All the late nights at the office, all the weekend trips... My skin prickles, and a tingle goes through me. He told me it was just once when I found him in bed with another woman; I try to breathe in deeper, but my throat is closing.

"You were given the paperwork, Julia. You signed everything."

I look up at Allen feeling betrayed by him, just as much as my husband. I want to question him, scream at him. But at the same time, I don't care. I had this coming to me.

I didn't know about this debt. I didn't know about the fucking apartment. I didn't know about a damn thing because I trusted them!

"I was mourning," I barely get the words out. They're cold and stagnant. Just a lame excuse for my ignorance.

"I'm sorry, Mrs. Anderson," he starts to say something else but I rise from my chair, a bitter taste in my mouth as I bite out, "Don't call me that."

He cocks a brow at me as I start to leave. "You need to sign these, Julia," he speaks to me exactly like my father does. Accepting my tantrum and simply telling me what I need to do.

My shoulders shudder as I open the door with my back to him and grip the cold brass knob for dear life.

"Email them to me," I tell him. "Email everything to me."

"I suggest you read them quickly," he tells me as I walk through the door.

I nod my head but I don't verbally respond; I don't trust myself to speak. I don't look back at him and I don't even breathe until I'm in the elevator. I can't relax though, even in the empty closed-off space. I want to sag against the wall, gripping onto the steel handles. I want to hit the emergency button and give in to the pathetic emotions threatening to overwhelm me. The sadness and betrayal.

But more than any of that, I want to see this fucking apartment. I want to look at where the hell my money went. I need to get my shit together and figure out how deep of a hole I'm in.

CHAPTER 22

Mason

She took everything from me, it's only fair.
I'll give it willingly, it's my penance to bare.
Forget the sins, let them stay where they are.
If she'll have me, I'll take her. But we won't get far.

KNOCK. *Knock. Knock.* My knuckles crack against Jules' door quickly, one after the other. I take a look around, shoving my hands into my pant pockets. The Upper East Side is far more traditional and full of old money compared to downtown where I live.

My father's only a few blocks from here.

Jules' street is different from where I grew up though. The cream stone and intricate carvings have history to them. Real history. I look back at the small iron picket fence and gate in front of her house. The city sidewalk is just beyond it, filled with people walking without a care in the world to wherever the hell they're going.

I rock on my heels and knock again, wondering what they think of this house.

It looks like incredible wealth and with the well-maintained garden and up lighting on the windows, it only adds to the beauty of the old home.

I've been inside Julia's home a handful of times now, and it's odd that I feel nervous about being here. But maybe it's because I'm coming through the front door in daylight. I smirk at the thought, but it's true. My forehead pinches as I knock again with the large iron knocker this time.

The door swings open and there's my Jules, but she doesn't stay there long. She leaves the door hanging open and disappears inside, muttering that she has to get something, but I didn't hear what. What the hell?

"Jules?" I call out after her, placing a hand on the heavy red door and peek inside after her. The door creaks and I second-guess going inside after her, but she doesn't answer me.

I take a few steps inside and flick the light switch on my right before shutting the front door. A large crystal chandelier lights up the large hallway. The ceilings are taller than they seemed at night. A pale blue and cream paisley wallpaper covers the upper half of the walls with a matching, but deeper blue below the chair rail molding.

It's modern and updated with a feminine and elegant touch, definitely not my taste, but it still holds the classic beauty of the home. A mix of modern and traditional sensibilities. It's all Jules.

"Jules," I call out again, pocketing my keys and wiping my shoes on the mat before stepping onto the plush area rug in the foyer.

"I'm sorry," I hear Jules call through the hall before I see her. She rounds the corner of what looks like the dining room, both hands on her left ear as she slips an earring into place. She's bare-foot, wearing a navy blue dress with white polka dots and a thin white-leather belt at her waist. She's gorgeous as always, but something's off. Something's wrong, although I can't tell what.

"Everything okay?" I ask her, staying right where I am as she bends down to slip on a pair of navy blue heels.

"Fine. Just," she shakes her head and stands upright, taking a step toward me before turning on her heels and heading back the way she came.

I follow her into the dark dining room. It doesn't look a damn thing like a dining room though. The furniture is all here, but a shitton of papers litter the table along with a laptop and a printer on the buffet.

"Sorry about the mess," she tells me in a dampened voice as she turns around. "I just need my purse and we can go."

She starts to walk past me, making her way for the door, but I put my arm out, my palm against the doorway and wait for her to look at me.

When she does my heart drops. Although her makeup is flaw-less, she can't hide that she was crying. Not from me.

"What's wrong?" It comes out as a question, but it's more of a command for her to tell me.

Her lips are the same dark red they were when I first met her and as she parts them, my eyes are drawn to them. She doesn't say anything though, she merely licks them and turns away from me. For the first time, deliberately disobeying me. Hiding from me.

"I don't want to talk about it," she says and starts to push my arm away, to leave me and deny me again, but I'm not letting this go. I grip her forearm tight enough that she stops and looks at me.

"That's not how this works. I told you before. If you're with me, you're with me." Her hard expression vanishes as I speak to her, replaced by nothing but hurt.

"You don't own me," she bites out the words meant to hurt me, meant to destroy the easiness between us.

"It's not about that, Jules." My voice is low as I release her. She doesn't fight me though; she stands there waiting for my next move. She knows how fucking good this is between us. She knows whatever the hell it is, I'll take the burden from her.

"I don't like seeing you upset," I say and bring my lips closer to hers. I can hear her heart beating faster. "Tell me what's wrong, so I can fix it." I open my mouth to give her a reason not to push me away, to tell her that she can trust me, that I care for her, to tell her everything I know she wants to hear, but I can't bring myself to do it. Luckily, I don't have to.

She moves her hands to her face for only a moment, her expression crumpling before she falls into my chest. That's my girl, she gives in to me so easily. I wrap my arms around her, feeling her shoulders shake and shudder with a soft sob.

"I didn't want to cry again," she breathes into my chest, muffled by the suit jacket and her hands still covering her face. She shakes her head as I bend down, running my hand up and down her back in soothing strokes and kiss her hair over and over again.

"It's alright, whatever it is, I'll take care of it." I don't know why I say that. It's stupid of me, and it gets the reaction it should from an independent woman like Jules. She pushes away from me, wiping under her eyes and taking in a shuddering breath.

"It's nothing you-" she closes her eyes and calms herself. "It can't be fixed." She glances at a photograph in a silver etched frame behind her on the wall and then wipes under her eyes again, walking to a large mirror on the far side of the dining room.

I only catch a glimpse of the photograph before turning my back to it. It's from her wedding day, and *he's* in it. Obviously. He was her husband after all.

Panic races through me, and a sick feeling churns my stomach. "It's about your husband?" I ask her, trying to keep the shame and guilt at bay.

She peeks over her shoulder, looking guilty. The fucking irony. "I'm sorry."

"Don't be," I say as I walk over to her, placing a hand on her delicate shoulder and watching her in the mirror. "Is everything okay?"

"No," she answers quickly and sniffles once. She's already fixed her makeup and looks as though she's back to pretending nothing's wrong, but then her eyes meet mine in the mirror. They're filled with anger and an unforgiving chill. "He had an apartment," she says with certainty. "A place for his mistresses or one-night stands or whatever the fuck they were."

I try to give her a look that expresses shock, but none of that is news to me. I wasn't sure if she knew. For the first time since meeting her, I feel guilty for not telling her, like somehow I could have saved her this heartache if I'd given her a piece of the truth. Only a piece.

She laughs something wicked and sad, a mix of both as she shakes her head and says, "You think I'm pathetic, don't you? A housewife who had no idea what her husband was doing behind her back." Her voice croaks and the strength leaves her with each word. I hate how she does this. How she blames herself, belittles herself. She's stronger than she knows. And worth so much more.

"What he did is a reflection of him, not you," I tell her as I take another step forward, standing behind her with her back touching my chest, just barely. "You aren't pathetic, Jules." I kiss the side of her neck, my eyes on hers in the mirror as I say, "I'd never think that."

"I do," she confesses. "He cheated once. He was so upset. He cried and swore up and down he'd never do it again. And I believed him. He lied to me!"

My heart beats erratically and I'm desperate to ask *who, who did he cheat on you with?* But I keep my mouth closed and wait for more from her.

"I really believed him." The pain comes through in her words as she turns in my arms, placing her small hands on the lapels of my jacket. Her eyes travel along the buttons of my shirt, her fingers shortly following. "I really thought he was good to me."

I pull away slightly, grabbing her wrists and getting her attention. "I'm sorry," I tell her with true sympathy, but it comes out rough and short, shocking her.

She pulls away from me abruptly. "I am too," she speaks to the ground, turning around and brushing the hair out of her face. "I think maybe tonight-" I can hear the excuse already; I can see her pushing me away, and I'm not going to let it happen. There's no fucking way I'm leaving until I know she's still mine.

Each time she questions me or what's going on between us, I feel like I need to hold her tighter. I can't let her get away without knowing who I am.

"Come here," I tell her barely above a murmur. She stops in her tracks, peeking up at me through thick lashes with a question in her eyes. She doesn't ask it though, she obeys me, taking two small steps back to me in those heels.

"He was a fucking fool to cheat on you," I tell her as I brush my thumb along her jaw.

She huffs a small laugh at me, and I didn't expect that. I narrow my eyes as she adds, "You're a well-known player, Mason." The humor vanishes and her smile fades to nothing as she adds, "You don't have to pretend to care. I'll be fine."

My chest tightens with anger, my heart racing. I won't fucking allow her to demean our relationship, too. "Bend over the table." I grit the words out between my teeth. I don't even think twice about it.

She merely blinks at me, shocked. She should have known better.

"Now, Jules," my voice comes out hard and I almost take it back. But this is the man I am, and this is what she's going to get. There's a war brewing between us, causing the air to suffocate me.

I need Jules for the woman she truly is, not this version that the memory of her husband brings back.

She holds my gaze for a moment and my heart sputters in my chest, thinking I'm going to lose her, but she caves before I even blink, submitting just like she wants to.

She braces her hips against the table, slowly leaning down to lay her upper body against the tabletop. That's the beauty of our relationship, she wants to give in to me. She desperately wants to trust and not be hurt.

"Lift up your dress," I tell her.

I hear her breathing pick up. "Mason-" she starts to question me.

"No, no talking. No excuses." I palm my dick, but I have no intentions of fucking her. This is all about pleasing her and showing her what she means to me. "Lift up your dress and show me your pussy." I crouch down behind her as she slowly pulls the cotton fabric up her thighs and exposes her lace panties.

My fingers trail up her thighs slowly, then to her ass, then up to the small of her back, pressing her down flat. I carefully push the panties out of my way, taking a languid lick of her pussy. My tongue brushes along the lace fabric and I almost rip them as I pull them farther away, but decide to use my fingers instead.

I play with her clit first, gently running my nail across the swollen nub and then back to her entrance. Goosebumps travel along her body. It doesn't take long for her to glisten for me, her wet folds begging for my attention.

She hums as she relaxes on the table, and it makes me smile into her sweet cunt.

It's going to be a slow build for her. I don't care about our dinner reservations. She's going to have deal with being late.

I use one finger, my middle finger, sliding it deep inside her as I stand up behind her, keeping my other hand on her hip. Her eyes are closed as I fuck my finger in and out of her, loosening her up and testing her readiness. I pick up my pace, remembering the anger and slip another finger into her.

"Come on, Jules," I say and kiss the back of her neck. "Tell me again how I don't care." A strangled cry leaves her and she whimpers an apology, still struggling to get away from the intense pleasure.

I push three fingers deep inside of her tight pussy, stroking against her front wall right where that bundle of nerves is and I don't let up as she screams out. She tries so hard to get away, pulling at the tablecloth and kicking one leg out, but I've got her pinned down to the table with my hip, one hand rubbing her nub ruthlessly, the other inside of her tight cunt.

"I would never cheat on you." And then I tell her words she has no idea how true they are, "I'd never take advantage of you."

"Mason!" she screams out my name, and her pussy tightens around my fingers. *Yes, my name!* I want her to cum screaming my name. To cum from what I do to her all because she let me. All she has to do is give in to me.

"Tell me you understand, Jules." I'm not letting her cum until I hear her say it. I swear to God I'll stop it all if she doesn't give me that.

I may be holding the truth back, but I'm not lying.

"Yes," she cries out as she thrashes her head.

"Yes what?"

"Yes, Mason."

I smile into her hair, slowing my pace and making her whimper as she desperately rocks her pussy into my hand.

"Yes, Mason what?" I ask her.

My heart thrums in my chest, but I need to hear her say it. I don't want that shit with her husband having anything to do with what we have with each other.

"You wouldn't do that." She bites her lip, looking back at me with a plea of mercy. "You wouldn't hurt me."

I crash my lips into hers and fuck her cunt with my fingers, relentlessly pressing against her hard clit. She cries into my mouth as her release hits her hard, and her hand bangs on the table as she tries to restrain her body from arching away from my touch. I don't let up, getting every single bit of her orgasm from her.

Her back bows with tremors of her release still rocking through her. This is how I want her, always.

No worry in her soft blue eyes, only a look of pleasure on her face.

A look that I put there.

My dick's hard as a fucking rock, but this isn't for me. She looks over her shoulder, still panting with her fingers gripping the cream tablecloth. She's waiting for me to take from her. To fuck her right here and now. But that picture of her husband is right there.

Part of me wants to do it. To force that beautiful cunt to spasm on my dick. To show her how a real man would treat her. But I can't. I need to get the fuck out of here.

I pull her hips back, her ass pressed against my hard cock.

Her lashes flutter and her wide eyes look back at me, waiting for whatever I have to say. "Dinner first, sweetheart." I kiss her lips gently, feeling her desperate pants for breath against my cheek, then brush her clit through her panties and smile as a tremor runs through her body and forces her head back against my shoulder.

I KISS the dip in her neck and then whisper in her ear. "Tonight."

CHAPTER 23

Julia

Naive and stupid, this shit has to end.
What did I think? I can't comprehend.
Mistakes belong where they're made, in the past.
I knew better, I knew this wouldn't last.
It left me numb, dead in the ditch.
Love is wrong, and my heart's a bitch.

I STARE out of the window of Mason's car as the city lights flicker on, even though it's not even dark yet. Classical music is playing as usual, and my body is still humming from the rush of pleasure he gave me moments ago.

But nothing is okay.

I need to end this. What's the saying? Get over one man by getting under another? I'm not interested for two reasons.

1. I'm not over what Jace did to me.
2. I'm not ready for another man.

That's what I've been telling myself all damn day. Ever since I left Mr. Walker's office. I don't have time for playing, and I'm not ready for anything serious. And that's what this has become, it's staring me right in the eyes.

This is serious. It's too serious. I feel like I'm fucking suffocating and what's worse is that the minute I'm with Mason, the very fucking second that he looks at me just right, says just the right things, the moment his lips press against mine and his skin touches mine, I'm done for.

I'm fucking head over heels for Mason. I didn't even hesitate to think if I should bend over my dining room table for him. I didn't hesitate in the garage either. He's had me from the very night we met.

There's something about him that makes me weak, and I'm tired of being weak.

I can't do this. I need to end it. But the very thought fucking hurts.

"I-" I start to give him the honest truth, my whole truth. Pressing my back against the seat and looking at him. *I can't do this anymore.* The words are right fucking there, dancing on the tip of my tongue. I don't know what's real and where I stand with anything and I just need space to figure it all out, but my phone goes off in my purse, the ringtone loud and obnoxious.

I let out a frustrated sigh, pulling it out and just missing a call from my mother. I almost call her back, but then I see the text messages. Dozens of them.

I hit the first one from Kat.

The last message makes me sick to my stomach. *It's going to be okay.*

What's going to be okay? What now? I scroll up, starting from the top.

OMG I just saw, are you okay?
Minutes later:
I can't believe he did that to you!
Everything is alright, we're going to get it taken down.

I DON'T HAVE to ask her what she's talking about. Maddie sent me a link to the online article. It's already been taken down, but she saved a screenshot.

My heart drops as I read it, but my eyes keep flickering to the picture. It's of me and Jace and right next to it, Jace and some beautiful woman. Scratch that. Some blonde bitch. It's obvious what the article was about, and it makes me fucking sick. My throat goes dry and tears prick my eyes.

Really? They fucking posted this shit now? I think back to who I told and who would have heard about the apartment. It's up for sale as of 4 p.m. today so that's a whole five hours it's been on the market. Motherfucking fuckers.

"Jules?" Mason's voice doesn't stop me from reading. It's not the worst thing that's been said about me, but it's not kind and it's not true either. I wasn't turning a blind eye.

My anger only increases when I see what they're saying about me now. I'm not running around town. I'm not spreading my legs... I can't even finish this stupid fucking article. They're claiming Mason's doing the same. And that I'm turning a blind eye to that, too.

Every fucking insecurity in me is replaced by raw rage.

I'm not this person that they're painting me out to be. I can't fucking stand this! I'm on the edge of breaking into a million fucking pieces.

Is that a stage of grief? Wanting to fucking murder everyone?

I just want to be alone!

I bite the inside of my cheek and whip the phone away from my face as Mason's hand lands on my thigh.

"What's wrong?" he asks me, his eyes darting from me to the road.

"Take me home," I tell him as I lick my dry lips. My heart hurts so fucking bad. I'm breathing heavily as I wipe my sweaty hands on my dress.

"What's wrong?" he asks again, and this time his voice is harder, the one he uses right before he turns me into a damn ragdoll and then magically fixes everything, but I don't give a fuck.

I'm done listening to men, and I'm done giving a fuck.

"What's wrong is that this isn't working for me anymore" I say in an even tone that splits my heart right down the center and immediately feel guilty. It's like slicing through it with a damn knife, the cut clean and quick, but the blood is pouring out so slowly and painfully. And I know it's not going to stop anytime soon.

I lean my head back against the headrest. "I just want to go home."

Mason's quiet, looking pissed off as he turns on his blinker.

The silence stretches between us, feeling awkward and horrific. What's really and truly fucked up is that I feel safe and happy with him. I feel like, if it were a different time, I could easily fall for him. I am easily falling for him. It's as if I'm falling down a well, but ever so slowly, time crawls and I'm able to look up, to admire the stonework, to casually look down into the black bottom of the abyss where I'll crash and die happily.

"I can't do this anymore," I tell him.

Mason glares at me and asks, "Because of a fucking article?" He grips the wheel until his knuckles are white. "I'll take care of it," and he starts to say something else. I'm sure it would put me at ease and fix all of my problems. He's so fucking good at that.

But I need to fix myself. I need to be whole before I can give myself so completely to someone.

"It's not the article," I tell him as my eyes burn.

"Is it your prick of a husband?" he asks with disgust so apparent I hate him in this moment. I confided in him about my departed husband and yes, he may have hurt me, cheated on me and lied to me, but that's not for Mason to judge. I still don't even know how to feel about it all.

"That's exactly why this shit needs to stop." My heart rages in my chest, hating me for spilling my guts, but I can't stop.

Mason looks as if I've slapped him. As if I've truly hurt him, but I can't stop.

"I'm not okay," I tell him feeling the burn in my eyes being dampened from the tears, but I don't care, let them fall. Let everyone see. "I haven't been okay, and I've been running from it. You can't come along and fix me. I can't just fall into another man's arms and forget about everything I'm going through."

I almost throw my phone out the window, the absurdity of my entire world crashing down around me feeling too overwhelming. I'm too hot, too angry, too miserable.

That's what it is. I'm fucking miserable, but aren't I supposed to be?

"Hey, stop," Mason says as he slows down at a crosswalk. "Just take it easy." His entire demeanor changes to something placating, as if he's talking to a wounded animal. It only makes me angrier.

"No. No, I won't stop. What do you want from me, Mason?" I ask him. And part of me is hoping he really is my knight in shining armor. Part of me wants to be weak. I want him to solve all my problems and just crawl into his bed every night, moving on to a new life and leaving the old one in shattered pieces behind me.

I know it's wrong, it's giving in and denying my responsibilities. But God I want it. My heart is suffocating, hoping for him to say just the right things to convince me to be his. Just like he has from the first night I met him. "What is it that you want from me?" I ask and my voice shakes.

"Jules," he says my name and looks at me with a gaze I don't understand and then he looks at me as if I'm broken.

"Just tell me right now, where is this going?" I try to swallow the spikes growing in my throat, but they don't move. They only grow larger, harder, and sharper and make the words scrape and hurt as they leave me. "I can't give myself to you right now unless..."

"Unless what?" Mason asks me, and it hurts so much because I don't have an answer.

I can't give myself to him unless this is forever, unless I can trust him.

But right now I can't trust anyone. The harsh reality is what truly does me in. I don't trust anyone anymore. I don't want to love anyone anymore.

I can't breathe as I take off my seat belt. My townhome is only a block away. I can see the iron gate. My hands shake as the seat belt pulls back, hissing and hating me just as much as I hate myself. My shelter. My sanctuary, and my grave.

"I can't," I breathe the words, feeling so fucking shitty. "I'm sorry," I whisper.

I unlock the door and push it open. A car's close but I close the door quickly, avoiding Mason's reach for me. His fingers brush against my back as I get out, just barely out of his reach.

"Jules!" Mason calls after me. I cross the lane, the car beeping and the driver holding down his horn.

I hear Mason get out of his car, leaving it parked in the middle of the road and already holding up traffic. "Jules!" he screams, but I keep running.

I push past the people and ignore the dirty looks and stares. My shoulders rise with a heavy breath. I just need to go home. Tears stream down my face. I need to take care of myself and figure out what the hell I'm doing with my life.

Tires screech and make my head throb as Mason drives alongside me.

I ignore him yelling at me as I whip open the iron gate. I don't stop until I'm safe inside my house, my back to the hard door, my body shaking and my heart hammering.

I hate myself for running from Mason.

But this is reckless. It was a distraction that turned into a fantasy of a reality.

I cover my mouth as another sob leaves me, slowly falling to my ass as I slide down the door.

He's a good man, and he deserves someone better than me.

Someone who doesn't have all these problems.

Someone who can fall for him freely and openly.

I sag against the door, curling my body and letting it all out, still hoping he'll come bang on the door and plead with me to explain. I can't be this person though.

It's the way we both knew it would end. I envisioned it would be him leaving me though, not the other way around. I take in a deep breath, feeling exactly how I should, like shit. Not that any of it matters.

It was never meant to be. And that's all there is to it.

CHAPTER 24

Mason

Caught between what you want, and you know.
Desperate for more, but struck back by the blow.
What to do, what to do.
When words will destroy,
There's no way up, and only hell below.

SEVENTEEN. I called her seventeen fucking times. It hurts worse knowing she left me for something other than the one reason she should. That I couldn't keep her on my own. I held on too tight. It's my own fucking mistake.

But I saw what I could do for her.

What I could do *to* her.

And that made me feel... something other than this. This fucking hate I have brewing inside of me.

IT WAS SUPPOSED to end this way. What the hell did I expect? I expected to keep her. For her to learn to love me. For that to make what I'd done right.

NONE of the reasoning and logic explains why I feel betrayed and alone. Not a damn explanation leaves me feeling as though this is something that doesn't need to be mended. The ice clinks in my glass I grab a bottle of Macallan Single Malt. The liquid sloshes in the bottle as I read the label, my fingers playing along the seal.

My father gave me this bottle as a gift when I started the company. When I told him I was going into business, but still doing what I loved. I felt so much fucking pride that day. My breathing quickens, and my grip on the bottle tightens.

Relax. I grind my teeth, feeling an uneasy tightness settle through my body.

Jules was a sweet distraction; how fucking ironic. She pulled me away from reality. She made me feel like I had time. Like I had a choice.

I toss the seal onto the top of my sideboard buffet, opening the bottle and not bothering to take a whiff before pouring it into a glass.

If my father was here, he'd give me hell for drinking it over ice.

"But that bastard's not here," I sneer under my breath. "No one is." The last thought leaves my chest feeling hollow. I take a long drink of the whisky, and it flows so easily. Burning and traveling through my chest, moving down deeper and stirring in the pit of my stomach. I take another, my head still tipped back and just finish the damn thing. The cold ice against my lips does nothing to numb my pain. I slam the glass down, a little harder than I should and let the liquor hit me.

But it takes too damn long. My eyes look straight ahead to the family portrait sitting on top of the buffet. This room, the dining room, is the only room in the whole damn place where there's a picture of anyone.

The rest of the house is devoid of anything truly personal. But what do I really have that's personal anyway? My lacrosse stick and all those fucking uniforms stayed at my parents' where they belonged. I'm sure they were thrown away long ago.

I pour the whisky into the glass, feeling my breathing slow as my body sways and I remember the first day I walked in here.

I'd just gotten all new clothes, all new furniture, all new everything. This home was the start of the professional version of me. All that was in the cardboard box I was holding was a handful of CDs, a few postcards from a friend of mine in Germany I'd met in college. We've lost touch since then.

My diploma was at the bottom, not that I have any real reason to hold onto it.

I take a sip, listening to the ice clack against the glass. The whisky sits on my tongue, and I press it against my teeth before swallowing. All of the awards I've won are in my office, framed and lining the wall.

My eyes drift back to the portrait of the three of us. I don't look a damn thing like her, like my mother. I'm the spitting image of my father, standing between the two of them. Mom's smile is soft, but her eyes are what sparkle. She was so expressive. Soft-spoken, but what she said, she made count.

She could make an entire room laugh by only speaking once the whole night. I let out a breath, looking at the firm hand my father has on my shoulder in the photograph.

He liked that about her. He told me once she was the perfect example of what a wife should be. That was before he caught her cheating.

I wonder if that man, the one she risked her marriage to sleep with, loved to hear her talk. I wonder if that's why she did it.

I down the whisky, pulling out the head seat at the table and sinking into it, my head leaning back against the crest rail of the antique chair.

This room is so fucking dark, with black textured wallpaper on the longest wall and the other three walls painted a soft grey. I wanted it to feel masculine. I remember telling the designer that. I told her I wanted it to feel like me.

On the right, centered in the room and next to the dark mahogany buffet is a long gas fireplace. With dark black crystals where the flames burn and sleek marble surrounding it. More black. Even the light fixture in the room is black. A circular pendulum that holds the light inside.

I huff a breath into the short glass and suck an ice cube into my mouth.

This is me.

A heart of fire that's never lit. A dark past that only holds a single moment of time in significance.

I wonder if that bitch designer knew what she was doing.

I kick the leg of the antique chair next to me. It's carved wood that's been smoked. The deep brown leather of the chairs has a worn look to it.

I fucking loved this room. I loved everything about it when I laid eyes on it. The only addition I made was that fucking silver picture frame, and then I filled that buffet with liquor.

And thank fuck I did. I raise a glass to the picture, even though my glass is empty, save for ice. "To you, you fucking prick," I breathe the last two words and take another ice cube into my mouth.

I crunch down on it, wondering if the toast was for my father or for me.

I push the glass across the slick table that I've never sat at for more than a drink or two and bring out my cell phone.

I fucking want Jules.

She's pure and sweet, and there's so much about her that I

want to keep. I really shouldn't have her. I've already been given more than I deserve.

"I can't do this anymore."

The screen lights up as I hear her words echo in my head. She shouldn't get to decide when it's over. Not like that. Not because of something so fucking stupid.

We work together. We make each other happy. I'm tired of living this life with nothing to fight for. I want her back.

My phone rings in my hand, startling me and making me drop it on the table. It vibrates, moving slightly as the ringtone goes off again.

I rub my eyes, feeling the heat of the drunken night start to take me in.

"Hello?" I think my voice is even. I'm fairly certain it comes out strong.

"Mason, we need to talk." I recognize Liam's voice immediately.

I rest my head in my hand and my elbow on the table before pinching the bridge of my nose. We do need to talk; we need to have a long fucking talk about how I can't go through with this.

All the money is spent.

But I can't keep pushing forward.

I need to give it all back to my father and cut ties. I need to turn him in.

Every bit of breath in my lungs leaves me, making my body feel light and my stomach sick. We're going to go fucking bankrupt without his money. But I can't be under his thumb any longer.

"We need that investment from your father's firm." A sad pathetic laugh leaves me as I register what Liam's said.

"We already have it," I say and stagger to the buffet, the phone on speaker, still on the dining room table as I pour another glass. The bottle's already halfway gone. "We've already spent it," I say loud and clear as I bring the amber liquor to my lips.

148

This time I inhale the sweet scent. Fuck, it smells as good as it tastes.

"We need more." I swallow the drink, staring at the phone on the table as Liam continues. "We got the estates on the Upper East Side, and the committee approved the demolition plans."

I shake my head and pinch the bridge of my nose again, setting the glass down. As I take a step forward, I start to regret having the last two drinks. My head feels groggy, and my body hot. "No, they didn't."

"I got it overturned. We've got everything approved, Mason." I can hear happiness in Liam's voice. Pride even. He claps on the other end of the phone, a rough laugh filling the room as it spins around me. "We just need that last check from your father."

I put both elbows on the table and breathe, "We don't need shit from him."

It takes a moment for Liam to respond, "What?" He took so long I almost forgot he was even on the phone.

"Are you drunk?" Liam asks me, the anger only thinly covered and I'm not sure why.

"No," I'm quick to deny it, but I know I am.

"What the hell's wrong with you?" he asks. "What's going on between the two of you?"

I shake my head, not wanting to answer.

"We aren't taking shit from my father," and it's all I can say.

"We are. We need those funds by Monday." Liam's voice is hard, but also panicked.

"We'll find someone else." My eyes narrow, and I steady my breathing. And my resolve. I refuse to owe a man like him. I refuse to play by these rules.

"By Monday?" He raises his voice and lets the disbelief ring through. "Mason, we can't. We'll lose the deal. It's not like no one else was waiting for this property. It took almost a year to get it."

Liam's voice starts to go in and out as he lists off every reason why this plan of mine is fucked. How we'll be ruined. How every-thing will fall around us.

I already knew it though.

I stand, leaving the glass where it is and the bottle of whisky still open, taking the phone and leaving the dining room.

"I don't give a fuck." I take a deep breath, listening to the silence on the other end of the phone. "I'm not taking another dime from him."

I have to face reality. Even if it fucking kills me.

CHAPTER 25

Julia

Nothing is suffocating,
It cuts off the air.
Nothing is drowning,
But nothing is fair.
Nothing to hold, and nothing to thrill.
When left with nothing, nothing can kill.

THE AIR IS crisp on the iron balcony. The thick oak trees just barely block the sounds of the city traffic. I've always loved the colors of autumn. The way the thick dark green leaves thin out and crisp up to gorgeous reds and burnt oranges.

They'll fall and waste away to nothing. Every spring they come back, good as new.

Bundled in my cashmere throw and sipping hot tea from the

thin porcelain cup that drips of wealth, I've always loved their pale green beauty. But not today.

It's not fair that they come back untarnished. It's not right that life continues after death... only for those deserving.

I let out a deep breath, calming myself and then twist the cap to the flask and pour a bit of tincture into my tea. A small, faint chuckle makes my shoulders shake slightly as the liquid mixes with the now lukewarm tea. *Tincture.* Vodka, really.

It used to be a tincture. It used to be just enough to take the pain away.

But sips turned to bottles as I preferred to feel numb.

And today is one of those days.

If I can just get out of bed and make it, the day will be okay. That's what I'd tell myself over and over again when Jace first died. Sometimes it's true. It's as if simply pulling the sheets tight and patting down the creases until they're all smooth is enough to hide the past and put the daily routine into motion.

Some days, it's all a lie.

All the time I spent with Mason. All that shit was just a lie. Some fantasy that life could be okay again. As if the crack in the glass didn't exist, or could somehow mend itself.

I take a sip of the tea, but it only makes my throat feel more parched. I set it down on the saucer and breathe in the cool air before covering my face with both of my hands. I press my palms against my sore, reddened eyes.

It's been so long since I've felt this empty. Since my heart has felt as though it's been torn open.

It doesn't make sense in the least. I was over him. I was making progress. True progress in healing by being okay with Jace being gone.

I was okay.

For the first time since his death, I felt like I had a reason to be happy. Like it was okay to be happy.

I look over my shoulder as I rub my tired eyes with the sleeve of my silk blouse. I thought I heard someone. Just for a second, I thought I heard a creak in the old floorboards, as if someone was behind me.

My first thought is Mason. That he's come back, and he isn't taking no for an answer. I roll my eyes, feeling my heart squeeze violently in my chest.

I can't make that more than what it was. A hookup, a fuck-buddy, I don't fucking know. But I know what it is now; it's over.

I settle back down in the iron chair and pick up the notepad. I haven't written a poem in so long, but there are scribbles every-where. Like loose poetry, lazy I suppose. It's a story. Of how Jace and I met when we were young. How we fit so well together, and everyone told us we were meant to be.

I close my eyes, remembering how the school bells would go off as we walked on the sidewalk to get to class. I brushed my knuckles against his, waiting and hoping. It had to have been obvious to him. Maybe I was the one to make the first move, but he chose me. He intertwined his fingers with mine, and he didn't let go. He was a good man, not a perfect man. But he was good to me. Or so I thought.

"Fuck," I utter the word beneath my breath and it comes out shaky. They say when someone dies, you remember the good times. But damn are the bad times there, too. And that guilt, that's something I don't want. I don't want to be angry at someone who will never have the chance to defend themselves again.

I feel like a bitch for scratching down the scenes of our fights in that notepad. I let the words flow and poured out all my fucked up memories. His infidelity.

I hear it again. I stand abruptly from the chair and as the iron scrapes on the balcony. I hear the creak of the floorboards behind me, and a chill sweeps down my body.

Every emotion that's made me a wreck washes away, quickly cleansed by fear. I turn slowly, my mouth parted but the words refuse to come out.

I don't have the strength or courage to ask who's behind me.

But I don't have to.

I let out a breath as a bushy tail comes into view.

"Boots," I say the neighbor's cat's name and add, "you bitch," with my hand over my heart.

She must've snuck in while the balcony door was open and I was busy mulling over my wretched life. There's an archway between my house and the neighbors, and Boots used to be a regular on this balcony. I take a few steps inside the bedroom and pick up the small tabby cat. Her fur is soft, and she purrs with content the moment I pet her. I only have a moment though. She gets fed up with attention quick and I've been on the ugly side of her claws before.

"You know you're not supposed to be in here," I scold her. Suddenly feeling exhausted, I walk her back outside, setting her down and shut the door just as the phone rings behind me on the bed.

The balcony is at the entrance of the bedroom so I have to walk quickly to get to the bed in time, but I do on the last ring.

"Hello?" I answer.

"Jules, how are you?" Kat's voice asks over the phone. "I was just calling to check in."

"A fucking mess," I tell her. My throat feels so damn tight. Is this what a breakup feels like? Or is this what regret feels like? I'm not sure which is which anymore. I suppose the two are one and the same.

"God, I know it's has to be rough." I nod my head, but my lips are pressed into a thin line.

"Do you want to talk about it?" she asks. I close my eyes and shake my head, and a moment later I'm able to tell her no. I'm composed, but only just barely.

"Hey, it's all going to be okay," Kat says as if it's a fact. "You know that, don't you?"

A small breath of disbelief leaves me. "No, Kat." I lie back on the bed and say, "No, I don't."

"Stop it. Stop it right now." Although her voice is harsh, I can hear the pain behind her words. "Not everything in life is good, but that doesn't mean you don't have a good life."

I lick my dry lips and close my eyes, lying back further on the bed and trying to relax.

"And you have a great life, Jules. You really do."

I hate that she can say that. Especially now when my life feels so empty and meaningless.

"I thought I was okay," I open up to her. "I thought I'd be able to move on. I thought I was moving on."

"You're going to, Jules." For the first time today, tears slip from the corners of my eyes as she speaks. I keep my eyes shut tight and hold my breath. "One day, probably sooner than you know, it's going to feel normal without him. It's going to feel good without him. And there's not a damn thing wrong with that."

"It doesn't feel like it's okay though. It doesn't feel like it's alright to not be upset." I shake my head, my throat feeling tight and hate that I can't explain what I'm feeling.

"It doesn't have to right now. You don't have to do anything right now, except tell me you're going to come to my house tomorrow night."

I sniffle into the phone, with a stupid smile that I'm sure looks ugly as hell plastered on my lips. I nod my head and I make sure I wipe every tear away from my eyes.

"Of course."

"Good, now… are you alright?"

I answer her honestly, "I'm not, but I think I will be."

"You *definitely* will be," she says with such conviction, even I believe her. My body feels lighter as I scoot closer to the edge of the bed, ready to do something.

"Do you want to go out for dinner?" I ask.

I hear her take a deep breath on the other end of the line, and I know she's busy. She's always busy with work. "I can't-"

"It's fine," I cut her off. "I've got to get out of this house," I tell her as I look up at the coffered ceilings in the bedroom. This house has too many memories in it.

"You go out and get some fresh air and maybe some shopping in, and I'll see you tomorrow night."

I nod my head. "You will."

"Love you, Jules." Kat's voice is soft when she tells me she loves me. It usually isn't.

"I love you, too," I tell her and it's so true. I'd crumble into a blithering mess without her.

As I rise from the bed, it groans slightly and I look back to find it a mess. I take the time to pull the sheets tight and lay the comforter just right. I even fluff the pillows and place them just where they're supposed to be.

As my feet pad against the old wooden floor, it creaks right where I know it should and that chill comes back to me. I look up at the balcony door and find it unlocked, which is odd. I swear I locked it. I go to turn the lock.

Click. It's loud as I stare at the lock, my fingers still on the cold hard metal.

I never did like having a balcony in the bedroom. Jace told me it was a silly fear. I cross my arms, feeling colder by the second and unsteady. I tuck a strand of hair behind my ear, grabbing my phone and clutch and throwing on a pair of faded blue jeans.

That's the feeling that's most recognizable, being unsteady. I'm not sure where I go from here. Worse, I don't know where I want to go.

But I know in this moment, with everything in me, I just want to get the fuck out of here.

CHAPTER 26

Mason

Tick-tock.
It's a bomb, not a clock.
Tick-tock.
It's about time to go off.
Tick-tock.
Prepare for the shock.
Tick-tock.
It's the truth to unlock.

I GRAB my wrist behind my back.

I stand at the window in my father's office on the other side of his desk with my back to the door as it opens. I watch as my cold grey eyes narrow in the reflection. The city traffic below is stirring with life, but it's silent up here. So many fucking people surround us, but not one of them can save me. Not one of them would even give a fuck.

Julia would. *My sweetheart.*

"Mason," my father calls my name and I turn to him, finally facing him and knowing I need to confront him and all this bullshit I've been running from. As much as I want to hold Jules close and pretend just being with her will make this right, I know it won't.

"Father," I greet him with a cold tone in my voice. Hating that this man is even related to me. I stare into his eyes and see my own. Everything about him reminds me of what I'm going to become. And I fucking hate it.

"We need to get over this," my father says and gestures between the two of us.

"We do." I clench my jaw, my heart beating faster. I stare down at my hands, ripping my gaze away from him. "I don't think there should be any more ties." It fucking hurts to tell him that. Even after all these years and everything he's done, I still feel pain at the thought of severing this relationship.

"Ties to what?" he asks.

"Between the two of us."

My father flinches as if I've struck him. But what did he expect?

"Watch your mouth." I can't believe he has the nerve to admonish me. As if what I'm saying is unspeakable.

"I want to walk away. I don't want to be tied to this anymore. I don't want to be associated with you." I hold my breath and wait for him to say something. I've played my cards.

"I'm your father, Mason. You can't walk away."

The fuck I can't. I bite my tongue, gritting my teeth as he walks closer to the left side of the desk and I walk around the right, a careful dance of power that escalates the conversation.

"You need to just forgive-"

"I'll never forgive you for what you did to Avery," I look my father in the eyes as I cut him off. Every muscle in me is wound tight, waiting for him to make the first move so I can destroy him and let out this rage.

His eyes flash with something. Anger, or maybe betrayal, but I don't know what.

"I did what I had to do to protect you," he says and pushes the words out between clenched teeth.

"She didn't deserve to be murdered," I seethe with anger. My hands ball into fists. Avery was a mistake. A fiery redhead with long legs, and a smile that could kill.

I met her late at night at an event, and I knew she was trouble.

I knew it that night, but I was in need of a quick fuck. She tempted me, and I took the bait. But I didn't know how it would end. I never could have imagined.

"That's what happens when you fuck with a Thatcher." My teeth grind as my father continues. "She decided to roll the dice. She's the one who came to me with demands and tried to blackmail us."

"You could have sent her to me," I point out and my muscles twitch with the need to pound my fist into his face as I take a step forward. "I would have told her the baby couldn't have been mine."

"If I'd known then-"

"You didn't have to know!" I yell at him, my throat feeling raw as the words are ripped from me, screaming up my chest and leaving me in a painful cleanse. "She wasn't innocent," I take a step toward my father and grab the edge of the desk to keep from gripping onto his collar, "but she didn't deserve to die."

"She did." My father's voice is hard, his back straight and his gaze full of confidence.

"She was pregnant!" I scream at him. Hating how he could so easily demean her existence. He had her murdered. He didn't even think twice about ending her life.

"With a married man's child!" my father screams back at me,

his face turning red as he leans in closer to me, and I can't take it any longer.

I can't take the arrogance and justification of ending a young woman's life so easily. I ball my hand until my knuckles turn white and punch my father in the jaw. His teeth crack and crunch under the weight of the blow. His head whips to the side as he reaches out to grip onto anything for balance, but it doesn't help him as he falls to the floor. He's limp and shocked, completely dazed. My arm stings with the pain of impact.

But it feels so fucking good.

He lies there for a moment, his hand over his mouth as trickles of blood leak from the corners of his lips. I shake my hand out, adrenaline rushing through my blood. I just barely restrain from kicking him in the ribs, from letting all of this anger and pent-up guilt out on him.

"You fucking prick." He spits blood out onto the floor and looks up at me with a menacing glare. "You choose some bitch over your own family."

No, I'm choosing what's right. I'm choosing to be better than this life I was born into. I don't bother to tell him my thoughts. They wouldn't do any good to him.

"Anderson didn't want that kid. Think about what she would have done to him!"

The mention of Jace Anderson makes me break my gaze. The memories come back and make my tense muscles spasm. I can't even hear whatever my father's yelling at me. It's all white noise.

I WAS BORN a Thatcher and I'll die a Thatcher, but I refuse to be anything like my father. Not today, not ever.

"I don't forgive you." I force my body to relax. I've said what I came to say. This ends now. "I never will." I walk out, the sound of my heart beating fast and my shoes smacking on the ground accompanying me.

Just as my hand grips the doorknob, I finally get the balls to ask him.

One last thing to say. One final question.

I turn to him, walking back to his desk with confident steps. He turns slightly from facing the window behind his desk, peering at me as if he doesn't trust me. And he shouldn't. Not with how I'm feeling in this moment.

I stop on the opposite side of the desk, my heart racing as I go back years and years. Back to a boy who lost his mother. Scared, confused... and angry.

"Mom didn't die from an overdose." The statement comes out accusatory, but it's meant to. He wipes blood from the corner of his mouth with the bright white sleeve of his dress shirt. He doesn't look me in the eyes, he doesn't acknowledge me in the least.

I take one step toward him, a large step that gets his attention. His gaze whips up to me. "You killed her?" I ask him.

"How dare you," he says and his nostrils flare as he pins me with his gaze. "How fucking dare you..." He doesn't finish, and his shoulders hunch forward as he grips onto his desk chair for balance.

I'm struck by the powerful way he's affected. I've wondered for so long, for months now. If he'd had Avery killed, maybe my own mother suffered the same fate.

I flex my hand and swallow thickly, feeling like I need to explain. It's a gut feeling more than anything else. I don't remember much around the time she died, but I remember how I felt, how the air between them was tense. How scared my mother was that he would find out her dirty little secret. "I know she was cheating-"

"Get out!" my father screams at me, not holding anything back as he throws his chair to the side, putting all of his weight into it. It crashes against the bookshelf, several texts falling down as he slams his fists against his desk.

I turn my back on him, my heart racing, my fist pulsing in agony from the punch and my chest hurting with a pain I can't explain.

He pounds his fists again and again as I see myself out.

Leaving my father and promising myself never to see him again, never to speak to him, never to trust him. And never to be like him. Never again.

CHAPTER 27

Julia

I asked for this.
I asked for pain.
I said goodbye to what caused shame.
They were watching,
And judging me.
But it's myself I have to blame.

I STARE DOWN at the neat piles of papers to my right in the dining room. My back is fucking killing me, and my shoulders are screaming in pain. It's wrong, so fucking wrong that now that this shit is sorted out my first thought is to call Mason, to see if he's free and tell him that I miss him.

He could ease the pain in my body, but also that sick lonely feeling I have after going through three years of finances.

Three years of hard evidence of Jace cheating. Three fucking years.

I glance at the email still open on my laptop. Mr. Walker will have more for me tomorrow. It makes my heart lurch in my chest, because I know I'll see more of this shit. I don't need to see it. That's the really fucked up part of it all.

I should and will sell the apartment and be done with it and all of the problems and loose ends that Jace left.

I'll be fine financially, and everything is going to be okay. But I want to know how long it went on for. I want to know at what point in my life I wasn't good enough for him anymore.

The wine in the glass is almost gone and it's late, but I pour myself another. We all have our vices and it turns out mine are Cabernet and Mason Thatcher. I take a sip of the sweet wine, my sad smile pathetic and weak.

I stare at the open newspaper on the table. The one with a photograph of Mason and someone else. Someone *new*. Fuck it hurts to see it, to think that he's moved on already. It hasn't even been two seeks since I saw him last. It has their picture, but the article is about me being left brokenhearted and used by the playboy bachelor. They know nothing, and I find it hard to give a fuck about what they all think.

But Mason. I've stared at that photo for far too long, praying it isn't true. Mostly because I'm a selfish bitch. I'm not ready to commit to him, or to anyone, but I want him all the same.

Sue has assured me it's bullshit and she's just some woman he dated long ago.

I take another gulp of the wine and look up when I hear my phone go off.

It's a text from Kat wanting my manuscript. Fuck my life.

It's a good thing I have an apartment to sell I suppose. Maybe I should thank my lying asshole of a husband.

I text her back asking for an extension, and then sit down to write. To let the words flow. If anything, I expect it to be about anger, grief, betrayal. But all that comes to me are thoughts of Mason's touch. How powerful his physical presence can be. How he can soothe my every pain. How he wants to, and about how much I want that, too.

I let my head fall to the left, exposing my neck as I remember him kissing me, as he played my body right here. I open my eyes and look down at the table where I bent over for him. I confessed something so real, so painful and he made me feel alive and as though it didn't matter.

I suck in a deep breath, hating that I left him the way that I did. But I'm so damn broken. I don't understand why he even wants me when it's so obvious I'm a wreck.

I bite down on my lip, picking the phone up and thinking of texting him.

I miss you. I type in the words and then delete them.

I'm sorry. I stare at the two words that mean so little, yet so much.

I think I love you. That's what I should send him. Scare him away for good.

I delete the text as Kat messages me back. She's usually hard on me, furious if I'm not on time with a deadline. But all she's written is that it's okay and to take care of myself.

"Take care of myself," I whisper beneath my breath and pick the glass of wine back up. I don't know how.

I wish Mason was here, but that's just an easy out.

This is supposed to hurt. It's supposed to be hard.

But God do I want to crawl back to him and beg for forgiveness. Beg him to take away the pain again. It's selfish and I won't do that to him, but I want to.

CHAPTER 28

Mason

It never ends. It won't go away.
One mistake from months past, will destroy all of today.

"I JUST GOT AN EMAIL," I hear Liam's voice as the door opens. His light grey suit is sharp and crisp, but he himself looks like shit. His ruffled, dirty blond hair is a mess on top of his head, and the dark circles under his eyes prove he hasn't gotten much sleep.

"About what?" I ask him and then rest my elbows on the desk, steepling my fingers and waiting to hear it. I know what the email is. My father's pulled the funds.

We're fucked. And I don't have a way out of this.

"What the fuck happened, Mason?" Liam asks.

I swallow hard, hating that I owe this man anything, but I do. At least an explanation, but what can I tell him? My heart clenches and I look down at my desk as I pick at my hands where a small cut mars my knuckles. I can't turn my father in. I don't have any evidence, but more than that, I can't bring myself to do it to my own father.

I clear my throat and lean forward to face Liam.

"We have to back down or find new investors."

"Back down?" He looks at me as though I'm the insane one here, and maybe I am. "We can't fucking back down. We've sunk millions into this!" I can practically see his heart racing out of his chest.

"I'm sorry, but-"

"What the fuck happened?!" he screams, throwing the papers on the desk behind him. My blood heats as I stare up at Liam.

"Sit down," I tell him. I'll take a lot of shit and I'll own up to failing him, but I'm not going to be talked to like that. He looks at me for a long moment and then he places both of his hands flat on the desk and leans over, getting closer to my face but still a foot away. Regardless, it's too fucking close.

"Don't fucking tell me what to do, Thatcher," he says, low in his throat. "This is going to ruin me. Ruin *us*," he hisses.

"We'll recover. It's just on hold." My voice doesn't reflect any of the confidence in my words. But I'll do whatever I have to in order to make this work. I have no intention of going anywhere. If I have to start from the bottom again, so be it.

"You need to get over whatever it is you have between you and your father." He nods his head, his eyes wide and bloodshot. "Whatever the fuck it is, just let it go."

He stares at me long and hard. He's waiting for me to comply, but it's not going to happen. I may not turn my father in, but I'm through with him for good. And I'm sure as fuck not going to take his money.

"I have a few meetings tomorrow with Marcus Jennings and Austin Hook." I sit back in my seat, daring him to come any closer.

His body tenses as he turns his head in disbelief, still leaning over my desk.

He shakes his head, still bewildered. "How the fuck could you do this to me?" he barely gets out. He pushes off the desk, shaking his head and walking a few feet away before looking back at me.

I can see each emotion as they flow through him and finally, he settles on anger. "Is it because of Anderson?" he asks me, and my heart stops in my chest.

I stand up straight out of instinct. Out of the need to figure out how much he knows.

"What the fuck does he have to do with this?" I ask him, my muscles coiled and ready for a fight. *What does he know?*

He flinches and says, "He?" He tilts his head, and it's then that I realize he was talking about Jules, using her married name. My heart sinks lower and a cold sweat breaks out over my body. Fuck!

"I'm talking about the bitch you've been fucking." My body turns to stone, stuck in place by an anger I can't control. Everything turns to red as he keeps going, oblivious to my reaction. "Everything's changed since she's come around."

I crack my neck to the side, deciding to ignore it. To give him one chance. That's all he'll get. "It has nothing to do with her."

"Oh yeah, she didn't convince you to make amends with your father? Or fuck him over or fuck me over?" With each question, his voice gets louder and louder.

"She doesn't know shit about my father, and she has no place here or in any of this."

He smiles at me, a cocky pissed-off grin. "Really gets you worked up, doesn't it?" He rounds the desk as he talks. "Is it because she dumped your ass on Madison Avenue?" he asks with a laugh and closes the space between us. I already know it's going to end badly; I'm just waiting for the right moment to strike at this point. "What'd you do that had her running out of that car, Mason? You fuck her over, too? Just like you fucked-"

I can't stop what's started. He shouldn't have brought up Jules. He shouldn't have done it. I can't control myself when it comes to her.

My fist comes out of nowhere, hitting him square on the nose and sending him flying backward. Twice in one week I've hit a man. And for the second time, I don't give a shit.

My knuckle flares where the cut is and my shoulder screams with pain from the impact. Adrenaline is making my heart beat faster and faster. I

take two steps forward with my hands up ready to beat the piss out of him, ready for the fight he obviously wants, but he's limp on the floor, blood leaking from his nose and dripping.

Fuck! I crouch down, my knee on the cold floor and grip the lapels of his jacket. He's heavy and unmoving. I fist his jacket in my hands, shaking him. "Liam!" Panic courses through me. I smack him hard across the face, leaving a red mark and sending a small splatter of blood flying, but he doesn't respond. "Fuck!" I drop him, and his head falls hard onto the floor.

I hold a hand over his nose just to make sure he's breathing. And he is, thank fuck. I stand up, running my hands through my hair and then down my face as I pace the floor.

Fuck! I look up at the clock and I only have five, maybe ten minutes before everyone gets here. I lean my forearm against the wall of windows, feeling defeated and like a fucking idiot. I lean all of my weight into it, my hot breath leaving fog on the cold window as the adrenaline wanes and the realization that I just knocked Liam out weighing down on me.

I stare at my own reflection as I realize how badly I've screwed things up.

I look back over at him, knowing I need to call an ambulance and that they'll call the police. I clench my jaw and swallow my pride. It'll be a fucking spectacle.

He shouldn't have talked about Jules though.

He had to know this was going to happen.

CHAPTER 29

Julia

Why do you haunt me so?
You take control of my thoughts,
You consume my sleep.
How do you wound me still?
You need to leave me alone,
I'm not yours to keep.

"IT CAN'T BE TRUE," I say without thinking. Sitting around the same small table in the coffee shop feels surreal as I read the article.

"You broke him," Maddie jokes to try and lighten the mood.

His company, his friendships, his father. I know the tabloids make shit up, but the mugshot is something that can't be denied. What the fuck happened?

"The charges have all been dropped and he'll be fine." Sue waves her hand in the air, blowing it off.

The newspaper falls to the table and the faint sound of the paper crinkling is all I can hear.

"I don't understand what happened." I think out loud. "He never said anything to me about his father or anything with the business."

Sue shrugs. "Sometimes people don't talk about that stuff. He'll be fine." She's good at shaking things off, but I can't. I don't know what happened, and I shared so much of myself with Mason. I was raw and open and gave him every bit of me. Obviously there's something he was holding back. *And that's an excuse for you to run back to him,* that snide bitch in the back of my head says, but her voice is different this time. She's coaxing me. I can practically feel a sharp elbow nudging me to go see him.

"Coffee?" Kat asks as she sits down and places a hot ceramic mug in front of me. It's the color of my cream accent pillows at home, very light from the almost offensive amount of creamer... just the way I like it.

I pick up the coffee and blow over the top, inhaling the smell and trying to feel normal. Kat's busy reading over the manuscript on her smartphone, but I don't even care.

She murmurs the lines as she opens up the book.

SWEET LIES YOU TOLD ME, *beautiful forever.*
  A dream or a terror, I craved it, whichever.
  A taste so sweet, too much to say no,
  I couldn't resist, and you couldn't let go.
  Your healing touch, and comforting kiss.
  But I never thought it would end like this.

KAT TILTS HER HEAD, her lips stopping mid-poem and she gives me a questioning look. "Is this one about Jace?"

The book was supposed to be about mourning and loss. And it is, but it's a deceptive cocktail of the two men. I loved and lost both of them.

I shrug my shoulders and take a sip of coffee. "I don't remember," I lie.

"So have you heard from him?" Maddie asks me, breaking me out of my thoughts.

I shake my head no. He got the message after I refused his calls repeatedly. I don't think he'll ever reach out to me again.

"Have you called him?" Maddie persists.

"Not yet," I tell her, not realizing the intention of my words. "Or, no. No I haven't."

Her voice is hopeful as she scoots forward, the sound of the stool scratching against the floor making an annoying screech. "You should," she tells me.

"I don't know. I want to." I trail my fingers up and down the cup and stare at a lone muffin in front of me. I haven't eaten since I heard about Mason this morning.

"I think you should," Maddie says softly.

"I think you should shut your mouth," Sue bites out and Maddie merely gives her a look of defiance.

"She breaks up with him and he falls apart-" Maddie goes off, but she doesn't get much out. What she does makes me feel like shit though.

"Stop it," Sue snaps. "That's not her fault." Sue points at the paper for emphasis as she says, "This has nothing to do with her."

"You don't know that." Maddie's response is soft as she looks down to her own blueberry muffin and picks at the top of it. "Everyone's saying he's heartbroken."

"Jesus, Maddie!" Sue scoffs.

"It's not like I was trying to hurt him," I tell her, my throat feeling tight. "I didn't think he'd care that much…" I don't know if that's true. I wasn't thinking of him when I ended it. I was only thinking of me. Of my anger. I take in a breath. "It just happened so fast, and it was too much."

"There's nothing wrong with fast," Kat offers. "Dave and I got engaged in three months."

It was a whirlwind romance, as they say in the novels. Picturesque in a lot of ways. But I had that, too. And it's over.

My heart begs me to stop, but I have to ask. It's fucking killing me. "Isn't it wrong? To fall for someone *else* so quick? After Jace?"

"No," Kat says and shakes her head. "It's wrong to turn something away because you're afraid of it though." Her voice is full of regret, but it didn't stop her from telling me exactly what she thinks.

"You guys are giving me whiplash." I groan and push the hair out of my face, resting my elbows on the table and burying my face in my hands. "I shouldn't be with him; I should be with him. I don't fucking know what to think!" I finally snap.

"What do you *want*, Jules?" Sue asks me. "Love isn't about thinking, it's only about what you feel." Of all the women in this group, I'm not sure I should take her advice on love, but she says it with such conviction and I believe it. And I trust her.

"I feel like I've been sad for too long." I tell her. "I feel like I deserve to be punished for moving on. I feel like I miss Mason. Like I hurt him," I brush my fingers under my eyes and suck in a breath to keep myself from falling to pieces. "And I'm a bitch for that. I feel like my life was spinning out of control and he was the one thing that was keeping me steady and I was taking advantage of that." I run my hands down my face and stare at the coffee in front of me, finally finishing my thoughts. "I don't know if I'm running away from all this shit or running to him." I swallow and whisper, "Maybe some of both?"

It's too much to take in and process, but I need all this mayhem to just stop.

"And you don't have to know. You don't have to do anything,"

Kat says. Her phone's turned upside down on the table and as soon as I notice that, I also notice all three woman staring at me with sympathy. Waiting for me. I don't deserve this. I don't know how I ended up so close with these women, but without them, I'd be so lost.

"You can take as much time as you need." Maddie says with a small nod.

That's the problem though. I wanted things to be slow, but he was a force I couldn't control. My body bowed down to his, and I would have been swallowed whole if I gave any more of myself to him.

It doesn't stop me from wanting him and the way I feel when I'm with him. He was right that first night, that he'd make me forget everything but his name and what he'd done to me.

"Are you sure it's not wrong? Because it feels like the worst kind of wrong." I look up at each of the girls, feeling like whatever they tell me will propel me in the direction I need to go.

"It's scary," Maddie says, shifting in her seat and breaking eye contact.

"Love is terrifying," Kat adds.

"It's not wrong. You haven't done anything wrong, and you should do what you want to do. Even if that's breaking every bachelor's heart in New York City." A soft, playful smile greets me as I look up at her. She nudges me and reaches for the paper. "This wasn't your fault though, but I can't say I'm not curious about the gossip."

My heart clenches in my chest. He never said anything about his father, or his partner. I bite the inside of my cheek, realizing maybe he was running from something, too. Maybe he wasn't running toward me at all. I just want to know the truth.

CHAPTER 30

Mason

Hurt and pain, they're for the weak.
Pathetic emotions, they never run deep.
Control and power are all they seek.
To numb you, to break you.
And leave you to reap.

ANGER MANAGEMENT. I crumple the paper in my hand.

No charges were pressed against me, but I'm sure Liam's getting a kick out of the anger management classes the judge recommended. Fucking prick. I know the asshole would have pressed the issue further if it wasn't for the company. He wants to save face and hold this over me so I can do his bidding.

That's not going to fucking happen. I'll take on all the debt if I have to. The project is canceled, so I'm taking the hit and dissolving the company. I drop the empty bottle of whiskey in the trashcan. The glass clinks against the metal frame of the photograph. I stare down into the bin, the shattered glass marring the photo of the picture-perfect family. It's destroyed... but really it had always been like that.

I'm tired and angry, and tired of being angry, too. I just want happiness. For me, that means Jules. I shake my head and lean back against the kitchen wall.

Call it what you want. Out of everything in life, she's the only thing I know I truly want. That has to mean something.

I start to make my way upstairs, walking slowly and dreading a night alone in this empty house. It never bothered me much before, but I can't fucking stand the silence now.

I stop midstep. *Knock, knock, knock.* Three times at the front door. I go still with my hand on the banister.

I wait a moment, wondering who the fuck would be here this late at night. I prepare for the worst, thinking it's my father. I can't face him right now. Not after what he's done and what I said. I open the door with a swift pull, prepared to turn him away, but my voice is caught in my throat as I look down at Jules.

Her baby blue eyes look at me with a mix of emotions. Fear, sorrow... hope. The chill of the wind spreads goosebumps along her arms and blows her long, blonde hair off her shoulders. She looks to her left and then right, pulling her leather jacket tighter around her and taking a small step toward me.

"Mason," she says and licks her lush lips. She's wearing that same color I've grown to expect from her. "I-" she clears her throat and looks away as I stand numb in the doorway.

Fate's delivered her to me. I can't let her go this time. I won't.

"I was hoping we could talk?" she asks me. Her heels click on the cement porch as she shifts with nervousness. Her tight blue jeans hug her curves, although the loose cream blouse beneath her jacket leaves much to the imagination. I know what's under there though.

I don't say a word, too afraid of scaring her off. Instead I take a step to the side and open the door wider, waiting for her to walk in.

Her cheeks and the tip of her nose are a beautiful rosy red from the bite of the night air.

She hesitantly steps inside and looks around as if she hasn't been here before. I close the door and stare at the lock a moment too long before turning it.

"Mason, I'm sorry," Jules' voice calls to me as I turn around to face her. I clench my jaw, watching her swallow and then bite down on her bottom lip. She's worried and apologetic, but I don't give a fuck about the past. I never did. I care about what she wants now.

"Why are you here, Jules?" I ask her in a rough voice. It's deeper than I intended, but it's all I can manage.

"I just heard about what happened," she says uneasily. She tucks her hair behind her ear and waits for my response, but I don't give her one. I'm not interested in talking about anything but us. I don't want to taint her with the bullshit. "I just wanted to say I'm sorry for hurting you," she says in a tight voice full of agony.

"Is that all?" I ask her, taking a step forward and closing the space between us. My heart thumps chaotically in my chest.

She twists her fingers around one another. "I also," she starts and then swallows. "I was wondering if you still... if you were interested..."

"In what?" I ask her, fucking hoping she says exactly what I want to hear. Make this easy for me Jules, and I'll make everything right. *I promise you sweetheart, I'll make it up to you.*

"If you'd like to maybe go out again? If that's what we were doing?" I stare at her a moment, thinking it's just too good to be true. She came back to me. There's a saying about that, but it's not meant for real life. It's not meant for men like me.

"If you still want me," Jules adds, the raw vulnerability so thick in her voice.

"I never stopped wanting you," I tell her and gently push her jacket off her shoulders. If she thinks I don't want her, she'll know better soon enough.

"Mason," she gasps as I lean down and kiss her neck. Maybe it's the alcohol or maybe it's just that my body knows hers. But I'm not waiting for apologies or excuses or explanations.

I need to *feel* her.

"Mason, stop." She pushes her hands against my chest, shrugging her jacket back on as I take a step back. "I need you to know that I'm worried we're going too fast. I'm worried that this isn't going to last."

I take in a deep breath and stare down at my sweetheart. "I told you, Jules. If you're with me, then you're with me, and that's all there is to it." I take her hand in mine and kiss one knuckle, then another.

"Mason," she whimpers as if I've broken her heart. She has no idea. I turn her hand over and kiss her pulse, my heart beating faster.

"No more of this running from me bullshit, Jules." I stare deep into her eyes, my heart beating loud and fast and erratically. "Are you with me?" I ask her, feeling more vulnerable than I ever have in my entire life. I whisper, "Are you mine?"

"I don't know that my heart is mine to give, Mason. It's broken, and I don't know if it will heal the right way." Jules sniffles and looks ashamed, but she has no idea how much I understand. I truly do.

Grief is a journey, and she doesn't have to do it all alone.

I wrap my arm around her waist and pull her into me. "You don't have to be perfect, Jules, to be perfect for me." I kiss her hair and hope that she can understand.

I tell her, "I want you how you are today, and tomorrow I'll want you how you are then."

Jules buries her head into my chest and murmurs, "Why are you so perfect, Mason? How do you know just the right words to say?" Her voice is soft and relaxed as she molds her body to mine, and that's when I know I've won her.

"I'm not perfect, Jules." My heart aches in my chest, knowing just how imperfect I am. And how imperfect I am *for her*. We aren't meant to fit together, but I'll force the pieces to connect and pretend it's meant to be.

For her. Because I owe her that much.

CHAPTER 31

Julia

I asked you to leave.
I need to be alone.
But you stayed in my head.
My heart and my home.
I asked you to leave me,
But you won't go away.
When I go to find you tomorrow,
I only hope that you'll stay.

MASON'S BEDROOM is so much darker than mine, full of deep greys and dark wood-tones. His curtains are thick velvet and shut tight. I can see him though, all of him. His muscles ripple over me in the faint light. It makes Mason seem so much more dominating, which is criminal.

He already owns me, consumes me with his presence. But right now, in this very moment as he towers over me, skimming his fingers over my sensitized skin, I'm weaker for him than I've ever been in my entire life.

"Mason," I murmur his name as he lays me down on his bed. I turn my head to the side and arch my back as he leaves open-mouthed kisses down my neck. We're both naked, but it's more than that. So much more. We've been here before, but this is different. We're bared to each other unlike we've ever been.

"If we do this, can you promise me one thing?" My heart is pounding in my chest because I feel like this is the end. It's putting so much to rest and moving on toward the unknown. I'm terrified that I'll go into freefall and he'll let me shatter when he's done with me.

"What?" he whispers between kisses.

"Please don't hurt me," I beg him. "I'll give you every bit of me, I promise." I can barely breathe. "But promise me if you want me to go, you'll let me down easy and as soon as you know." He braces his forearms on either side of my head and looks down at me with an intense look in his grey eyes that pierces my lungs, stopping me from breathing.

"You need to stop this." His voice is hard, but it always is. "Do you understand?"

My heart stutters and lets me speak as I struggle to nod my head. "Yes." And I really do. I want this to stop and for *us* to begin.

"Don't hide from me, Jules. Don't run from me," Mason tells me with an authority that can't be denied.

I nod my head in complete agreement. I'm tired of running and denying myself what I really want. "No more secrets," I whisper into the hot air between us.

Mason pulls away, looking at me as if he's going to tell me something, taking me in and making the silence and tension grow, but no words come. Instead he crashes his lips against mine and pushes his body against me, forcing me to spread my legs for him.

And I do, I let him have all of me.

His fingers trail along my pussy as my core heats. He doesn't stop nipping and kissing over my heated body, his hands roaming freely, taking in every inch of me. I'm helpless beneath him. Falling deeper and deeper into the darkness, and loving how overwhelming it all is.

He groans in the crook of my neck, a sexy deep sound that makes my body arch toward him as if drawn even closer to him by an undeniable pull. Our skin brushes against one another as he pushes himself inside of me.

My mouth opens and I stare up at him, his grey eyes holding my gaze as he enters me, slowly stretching me and not stopping until he's fully seated inside of me.

My heart beats faster, my body is numb and on edge, waiting for him to move and take me how he wants me. Rough, raw, and making me *his*.

His fingers dig into my hips, pinning me down as he pulls out of me slightly and then slams back in, forcing a whimper from me. My body bucks instinctively, but I never break eye contact. I can't. He holds me captive beneath his gaze.

He does it over and over again until I'm so wet and hot for him that he slips easily in and out, each time forcefully smacking against my clit.

My body writhes and begs me to move away; it's too much, too intense. But that's just how Mason is. I knew it when I met him, and I want him still. More than that, I need him. I need this.

He groans low in his throat as he speeds up his relentless thrusts, resting his forehead against mine and kissing me mercilessly. Our lips barely touch, but they do, over and over again, meeting in a slow kiss with our hearts racing.

He steals the breath from my lungs. His hot body makes mine

burn with desire. I cling to him, wrapping my legs around him and digging my nails into his shoulder.

He pushes me higher and higher.

The pleasure comes in small waves, dim at first but growing increasingly stronger. They threaten to overwhelm me as my fingers and toes tingle. The crash will shatter me, I know it. I don't beg him to stop. I don't try to pull away. I want it, I crave it, and I'm desperate for him to ruin me.

"Mason!" I cry out as the wave consumes me, pulling me under in an intense orgasm that paralyzes my body. It's Mason's cue to devour me, and he does, fucking me with no regard for the state I'm in. He's chasing his own release, pounding into me recklessly and extending my pleasure that much longer.

I scream out as he whispers, "Mine," in the crook of my neck again and again. His voice gets louder as he fucks me harder and harder. My lips won't close and I can't do a damn thing but take everything he's giving me. And I do. His large body is suffocating me in the most delicious way.

It's only when he stills deep inside of me as I pant under him, desperately trying to breathe, that I'm able to moan out my pleasure. His thick cock pulses, and the wetness between my thighs leaks between us.

He doesn't stop holding me.

He doesn't stop kissing me.

And I almost don't tell him. I almost hide from him, but I promised him I wouldn't.

"I love you," I whisper and give that piece of me to him, too. He doesn't say it back, but I know he heard it.

He kisses me without mercy, soothing my pain and taking everything I have.

CHAPTER 32

Mason

I know what I want.
I know what it will take.
I'll push the limits till they break.
You can't deny it.
You can't pretend.
You were meant for me, until the end.

HOW LONG IS LONG ENOUGH? I keep thinking it over and over again. As if I'm not a fucked up fraud for asking Jules to marry me.

It's been two weeks of us falling perfectly into place. She's still waiting for the other foot to drop. For this fantasy we're living to crumble into pieces. I won't let it though. I'll give her everything she wants and that includes a ring, a sense of security that will seal us together and truly put our past behind us.

My eyes focus on the deep red petals scattered on every

surface. I want her, and I don't give a fuck about anything else anymore.

The only thing I give a damn about is making Jules mine in every way.

I don't want her to tell me no. I can't stand the thought of her turning me down or worse, if somehow just asking her to be my wife could push her away. It's happened before, and I'm terrified to send her running again.

It doesn't matter how fast she is though, how quickly she'll turn me down and try to hide. I'll find her, I'll catch her and I'll wait for her. Always.

I close the small, black velvet box, making the vision of the four-carat, cushion-cut diamond vanish and shove it into my pocket. Letting a heavy breath leave me, I turn and look at the living room. It's fucking obvious. So damn obvious that I'm going to propose.

The second she walks in here and sees the crystal vases of deep red roses on every surface, she's going to know what's going on.

I can see her now, standing in the doorway, gripping onto the frame while her doe eyes go wide and she breathes in the floral scent. The lights are low and the tea lights are scattered around the room.

I'm not a romantic man by nature, but for her and for this... Hopefully for the start of our lives together, I can do romance. *All for her.* I'll pretend to be someone else until both of us believe it.

At the sound of the doorknob turning, my heart skips in my chest, hammering harder than I anticipated. I take a step back, pulling the box from my pocket and preparing myself to get down on my knee. My blood heats, and anxiety suddenly washes through me. It's really happening. I'm really going to ask her to marry me. The thought itself calms me.

Of course I am, *I love her.*

I run my hand through my hair and shift on my knee as she steps forward enough to come through the doors. I thought she'd be astonished by the sight of the room. I imagined her taking it all in, but she's only looking at me.

"Julianna Lynn Summers, I would be honored-" I start, and already I've fucked up. I had this damn thing rehearsed. I thought I had this shit memorized, but having to look up at her and not knowing what she's going to say fucked me up.

Jules covers her mouth with a gasp, letting the front door close shut slowly behind her. Her shoulders hunch forward some as her purse falls to the ground. I knew she'd be emotional; I just wish the shock would wane so I could see which side of her was winning out. The side that loves me and wants to live in the moment, or the side stuck in the past and afraid to move on.

Jules takes a few steps forward when I don't continue, her thin heels clicking on the polished wood floors as she places her hands on my shoulders and starts to lower herself to the ground, but that's not how I want her. I wrap an arm around her long legs and look up at her, still holding the ring out although she's staring into my eyes.

"Jules, I love you and I want to spend every day of my life with you." I hesitate to say the words, but I have to, even if she says she can't. "I want you as my wife," I say and watch her facial expression crumple with a hint of pain reflecting in her eyes as I say the words.

"I love you too, Mason," she barely gets the words out as she covers her face with both of her hands and then wipes under her eyes. Her eyes are glassy with tears and her voice choked as she says it again. "I love you, and I didn't know if I could ..." Hearing her start her confession breaks my heart, and I get up off of my knee to hold her. She wraps her arms around me, squeezing me as though she needs me to stand. And in so many ways she does. She needs someone there, and I'll always be that person for her.

So long as she'll let me.

She pulls away slightly, trying to pull herself together as she brushes her hair out of her face and looks away, taking a calming breath, but that's not the version of her I want.

"I want all of you Jules," I tell her as I cup her chin in my hand and force her to look at me. "When you're upset, I want to know so I can make you smile. When you're angry, just tell me, and I'll let you take it out on me however you need, then make you cum so hard you forget you ever felt anything other than bliss. I want the real you. Always. I never want you to hide from me."

Those lush lips part and a soft breath escapes her as she stares into my eyes. She's searching for something. She better not fucking wonder if everything I've just said is true or not.

"I want the same from you, Mason." I'm surprised at her response. I stay still on the ground, wondering how she could think for a second I wouldn't share all of me with her. Not my past. She doesn't know shit about that, and she never will. None of it. I'm going to fix it all and keep it hidden in the shadows and buried deep where it all belongs.

She kneels on the floor in front of me and takes my jaw in both of her hands, planting a soft sweet kiss on my lips. Her touch calms all my worries. It rids the demons threatening to surface. She does this to me. She makes me a better person, and I desperately want to be that man for her.

She speaks with her eyes closed, her lips close to mine and her hot breath filling the air between us. Her long, thick lashes are damp with her tears as she tells me, "I love you for you. The good and the bad. And I do want to be with you, Mason." Her voice is pained and I can't help but reach up and hold her, pulling her closer to me. "I need you," she whispers.

I kiss the crook of her neck. "All I need is your love."

"You have it Mason, you have that and me and my life..."

She still has yet to answer; I need to hear her tell me yes. I want to be good enough to be her husband and if I'm not today, then tomorrow I'll be better. I'm determined, and she needs to know that. I put my hands on her shoulders, brushing the fine lace of her blouse so I can look at her when I ask.

"I love you, Jules. Will you marry me?" I ask her, looking deep into her eyes.

She gives me a sweet smile, almost a shy one as she sniffles and finally gives me everything I need. "I love you, too. Yes." Her words come out as if it's obvious. As if it's only natural.

I finally breathe a deep sigh of relief, heaving in the air and holding her close to me. I stand up, still carrying her and swing her in my arms as I rise.

I kiss up her neck and every inch of her exposed skin, making her let out a small, feminine laugh and push away from me slightly. This is the only kind of pushing I ever want her to do again. From this day forward, she's mine.

I only set her down so I can pick up the ring from the box. I watch as Jules' eyes widen once again. "Oh my gosh," she says softly, eyeing the ring as though it's the most beautiful thing she's ever seen.

"Do you like it?" I ask her as I slip the box into my pocket and hold the ring out for her.

She bites her bottom lip as she nods vigorously and says, "Mason, it's beautiful." Finally, she looks up at me as I slip my ring onto her finger. "I love it," she whispers.

A small breath leaves her as she rubs her fingers over my five o'clock shadow and gently kisses me. I've never felt anything like what I feel for her. Seeing my ring on her finger makes it seem as though it's all going to be alright.

As if the past will stay buried where it belongs.

CHAPTER 33

Julia

Lies lies go away,
The sins were all from yesterday.
We tried to run, you tried to beat us.
Now we're ruined, left defeated.

THE FRAME CLICKS INTO PLACE, and I turn it over in my hands and smile. I straighten my back at the bar stool and hold up the heavy silver frame. This isn't for hanging out here where everyone can see, and it's silly really, but I wanted it framed.

My engagement ring clinks against the frame as I hold it up, the sunlight from the large bay window in Mason's house--well our house now, reflecting off the glass as I read the words.

A New Love and New Beginning.

It's the first article of us that was run in the papers. Back when I didn't know how to feel about the two of us, when I was riddled with guilt and pain and not seeing things clearly, I hated that we were in the papers at all.

I happened to come across it online the other day and when I read it, I lost it. Mason had to come in and find out why I was crying. He's always worried that I'm going to break down. I wish he wasn't so concerned for me. Something as simple as this article shouldn't get me so emotional, especially since half the facts aren't even true. But I love that our story has a beginning that was captured. I love that everyone around us knew.

I never would have thought that this article would give me pride and bring back a memory I want to be reminded of. A night when two lost souls knew they needed each other, even if we were too blind or stubborn to see it, *we felt it.*

"Finally," I say with a bit of pride. It's framed and perfect, just how I wanted it.

I hear Mason's rough chuckle as he walks into the kitchen and wraps his hands around my hips and then plants a kiss on my shoulder.

I have to close my eyes as he hums and places his hand on my lower belly. He wants a baby. The very thought warms me and makes my head fall back against his broad chest. Wedding first though.

"Soon," I say softly with my eyes closed.

"What's this?" Mason asks, picking up the frame and reading the article. I watch his eyebrows raise as he reads the article.

"I was going to put it on my nightstand," I tell him softly, waiting for his reaction. I'm still adjusting to moving in. I'll never sell my family home, but I'm happier here, away from all the reminders of what used to be.

Watching Mason recall how we started makes me nervous. We went through a lot that isn't conventional, and I still get a little insecure about it all.

He sets the frame down and kisses me again. It's soft and sweet, but it lasts. My heart swells each time he kisses me like this. When he pulls away, he grins at me. It's a cocky one that lets me know he thinks he's got me all tied up in knots. And he does.

"Why this one?" he asks.

Truthfully, I'm not sure I can vocalize why I want this particular one on my nightstand, so I just shrug.

"I just want it," I tell him simply and my easy response makes him smile.

"Well if you want it, then it's all yours," he answers me.

And that right there is why it was so easy to fall for this man. It's simple and natural. No rhyme or reason. It just feels right.

The frame clinks on the counter as I set it down. It's a lazy weekend and I really have to write to get this manuscript in before the deadline, but I'm doing everything I can to procrastinate.

"Do you a drink?" Mason offers. He has a sexy grin on his lips and I know he wants to stay in and do bad things tonight. He likes it when I'm tipsy, like the first night we met.

I can't resist him, so I nod my head and his smile widens, filling me with warmth. I'll never get enough of him and how he makes me feel.

I push the frame away and pick up the first envelope from the pile of mail sitting to my right as he heads to the fridge. The envelope tears easily and a handwritten letter slips out.

I feel my brows bunch as I unfold the thick cream parchment. Who the hell sends a letter like this in a plain envelope? Before I read it, I check the envelope again. My name is there, but no return address.

My eyes flicker to Mason's back as he rummages in the fridge and then back to the paper.

Dear Julia,

It pains me to tell you this, but I can't stand to watch from a distance as you fall into a trap. Your husband was murdered. I know this is going to shock you, but I have proof. You may not believe me, but I pray that you do.

Mason Thatcher murdered him. Don't trust him. Don't let him know that you know. If he finds out, you won't be safe.

There's more, but I can't read it. A shiver rolls through my body and everything seems to blur.

My heart thump, thump, thumps. My body heats so fast. I reread the words, blinking and taking it in. My lips move with the words, but I can't breathe. I can't focus.

The handwritten letters seem to swirl together into a cloud of distrust. My vision fades, and I feel so fucking dizzy. I back up slowly, pushing away from the island and letting the feet of the stool scrape against the tiled floor. Mason looks up at the noise and my weak legs barely hold me up as I grip the stool, my bare feet padding against the cold ground.

My head shakes on its own. That's not true. It's not true. It can't be true.

"Jules?" Mason's voice is riddled with concern and something else. Something I never registered before, but I can hear it now. I can see it in his face as I barely breathe and look up at him.

"The-" I can't even speak the words. It's a lie. It has to be a lie. What a cruel fucking lie it is. But Mason's response is throwing me off.

He sets a glass bottle of beer on the counter, squaring his

shoulders, all humor gone from his face and something else, *someone* else, stands in front of me.

"Mason?" I barely get his name out.

"What is it?" he asks me in a voice so menacing, I'm scared. No. I shake my head. "Mason, no," I say, and my throat goes dry and my words crack.

This isn't real. My fist grips the stool tighter, and I struggle to react. This is a fucking nightmare. It has to be.

I'm caught in between my need to run for my life, and the need to know the truth. I need the truth. No more lies; no more secrets.

"Did you do it?" I ask him weakly and in an instant, something snaps into place. As if he's acutely aware of what I'm saying. As if he's been waiting for this.

No. My body turns to ice, my blood and lungs freeze and I can't believe this is reality. It can't be true.

Mason takes a step forward, around the island and it breaks me from my denial.

It's my cue to run, a natural instinct that takes over. The stool falls hard, crashing to the tiled floor as I take off, but Mason's faster, gripping my wrist and flinging me backward. I cry out from the pain shooting up my arm and he releases me only for me to fall onto the floor.

My heart pounds in my chest. *Thump, thump, thump.*

"Did I do what?" he asks me, his eyes narrowed and cold. This isn't the man I know.

My bottom lip wobbles, the small bit of strength vanishing as I take in the raw truth. "Did you kill my husband?" The words feel as though they claw and scrape every inch of my throat as they come up, leaving me damaged and in agony as they float in the tense air between us.

I can't believe I even asked him that. *Deny it. Please deny it. Tell me I'm stupid and heartless and a fool. And this, whatever this is, it's something that's already over and never happened.*

Mason stands up straighter, giving me enough space so that my breath could come back to me, but my lungs refuse to fill until he answers me.

"They think they can do whatever they want," Mason says ripping the paper from my hand and standing over me. I didn't even realize I was still holding it. I can't move, I can't breathe. This can't be true. It can't be.

"Your husband wasn't a good man," he says low, deep and rough, his eyes piercing into me before flickering back to the paper. He crumples it in his fist as my body heats and a cold sweat spreads across my skin.

"No," it's all I can say. "You didn't," I try to speak. I don't know if it's shock or if I'm just that pathetic.

"I did." Mason's confession makes me lightheaded and sick. So fucking sick.

My heart twists with a pain that's unbearable as I turn onto all fours and try to run. Crawling as quickly as I can before I can stand. The bottom of my feet are sweaty from nerves and I slip against the ground, crashing hard to the cold, unforgiving floor.

"No!" I scream out at him, leaving a strangled cry of a sob to linger between us. It's only then that I even register I'm crying.

I try again to run, managing to get to my feet, and the door is so close. I scream out, although I doubt anyone could hear us. Not here in Mason's home. I practically slam into the front door, but Mason's right behind me.

With one hand on the front door and one on the knob, his hard body presses against mine, trapping me between him and my only escape.

His large body cages me in. I'm left facing the door, barely able to stand or breathe. "I'm sorry, you were never supposed to know," he whispers as he braces one forearm to my right and the other to my left. I shrink beneath him, the weight of the reality crashing down on me.

I've fallen in love with my husband's killer. I've slept with him and given him everything.

And now he has me at his mercy.

"I'm not going to hurt you, Jules." His hot breath sends shivers down my back as he adds, "But I'm not letting you leave."

CHAPTER 34

Mason

I couldn't think, I couldn't breathe,
I couldn't see past the red.
I knew the risks, and it was wrong,
I didn't stop till he was dead.
I can't go back, you can't pretend,
I never wanted you to know.
But pain and betrayal are all that's left
There's nowhere else to go.

TEN MONTHS *earlier*

ONE MORE CONTRACT, *and then we just have to get the land converted to residency. The last name on the list is Morgan & Summers, a realtor* company although they also do investments and developing. They'll be the hardest to sell since they're competition.

I rap my knuckles against the maple door of the owner's office. I expected Howard Morgan, but the man who opens the door doesn't look a damn thing like him.

He's tall and young with thick blond hair cropped short, not the old man who's owned the company for nearly fifty years. That man I was ready to sell the proposition to; no children and retirement within sight. I could have had him signing the papers within the hour.

Two green eyes narrow at me as the man holds out his hand for a firm shake. As soon as I slip my hand into his, a polite gesture, the man puts his other hand on top and smiles.

"Mason Thatcher," he says as he holds the handshake.

My brows bunch and my muscles coil. "You have me at a disadvantage," I say politely although my voice is low. "I was expecting Mr. Morgan."

The man releases me, the smile still on his face. He gestures for me to enter, and closes the door as I do just that. It doesn't escape my attention that there are two desks in the large open office. One on each side of the room, mirroring each other, both large dark wood, shining with a fine polish.

I was under the impression that Mr. Summers has stepped down. Apparently someone else has stepped up.

The windows are floor-to-ceiling, filling the room with bright light. It's new, modern and it's just then that I realize changes have definitely been made to this company that haven't been made public yet. And that could fuck up this sales pitch.

"Jace Anderson," the man says as he straightens his tie and takes a seat at the desk on the right. My blood chills as the name registers.

Jace Anderson. I stand there for a moment, my grip on the briefcase tightening as I struggle to comprehend how I'm in a room with this man.

He's the other man Avery slept with. The other man she blackmailed. The man who knocked her up.

My eyes dip to his hand as he picks up a manila folder and opens it. His wedding ring is in plain sight.

My heart rate speeds up, but I move quickly to take the seat and pretend like I have no idea who he is. I don't know what he knows. I sweep my hand over the back of my neck, hating how my collar suddenly feels tight. I look anywhere but in his eyes.

My father had her murdered Jace's child included. It's all I can think about as the man speaks about terms and how he'll be handling the deal from here on out.

He doesn't seem to know. If he has any idea about how Avery died, he must not know my involvement. Not that I knew about anything until it was over. I know she was killed and I have good reason to believe my father was involved. I don't have the fucking balls to ask him. He told me about her blackmail attempt, and I know he wouldn't have sat by and done nothing. But that baby wasn't mine. It was Jace's all along.

*"M*R. A*NDERSON," I say and clear my throat and stand abruptly. I can't sit in the same room as him, caught off guard and thinking about what happened and the unfortunate connection between us.*

"Forgive me, but I need to reschedule." Anderson stands up with me, fastening the bottom button of his suit jacket. "I do apologize," I tell him evenly.

His brow bunches as he looks away from me. "You weren't expecting me, I take it?" he asks.

I shake my head once, holding his gaze. "I wasn't."

He scratches the side of his neck casually before asking, "It's not because of the redhead?"

His question catches me off guard once again. Avery. I still from his question, my heart racing a mile a minute, although on the outside I'm cool and collected.

"When I told him I'd pay for half, I didn't mean right then and there." He shrugs, not looking at me, but staring out of the window as he shoves

his hands into his pockets. *"I'll pay him,"* he says and looks at me with a grin on his face, *"when I feel like it."*

Adrenaline races through my blood and every hair on my body stands on end. Pay for the hit?

"Is that so?" I mutter beneath my breath. Money for the hit. He knows. That's the only logical thing that makes sense. Here he is smiling and withholding payment for a hit on his mistress.

"When did he ask you?" I ask him evenly only to get more information from this prick before my anger gets the best of me. I need to know who he is, and I need to make sure I'm hearing this right.

"I mean, I knew before it happened, but your old man didn't tell me when." The smile dips from his face for only a moment. *"If he hadn't joked about waiting till she'd told my wife, I'd be more... amenable."* My old man. No. I grit my teeth and suffer through keeping eye contact with this asshole.

"Told your wife what?" I ask him, and the lie in my voice comes out so naturally even I believe it. *"About the baby or the affair?"* It's as if I'm truly curious and not disgusted in the least.

"Does it matter which?" he says easily, moving back to his desk and taking a seat. *"Like I said, I'll pay him when I decide to. If you decide to hold up business, that makes no difference to me. We'll find a different developer. There are plenty that want this property."*

What I want to do is beat the shit out of him.

I give him a tight smile and reply, *"You'll hear from me soon."* I move toward the door, each step harder and harder to take. I'm only able to manage my anger because I know what I'm going to do as soon as I get to the parking lot.

I'll watch which car is his. I'll follow him. And I'll make him pay for what he did.

None of these assholes care who they hurt along the way. Him, my father. All these high-powered pricks I deal with every goddamn day. Life means nothing to them. They get away with murder and corruption, never paying for their sins. But Anderson... he'll pay for it.

Avery made a grave mistake, but so did he.

YOU CAN'T CUT the breaks in a swift, clean stroke. It has to look natural; there's a technique to making it look like it was an accident.

I didn't even think twice.

Yes, I killed her piece of shit husband. I set him up to die, and I don't give a damn that it happened exactly how I wanted.

The bastard had it coming to him, but Jules was never supposed to find out.

Someone knows. The knowledge brings a chill to my body. Someone knows what I did. It's been ten months. So much time has passed, and yet they've said and done nothing.

I hold Jules closer to me as I drag her up the stairs. The shock is over, and now her instincts are kicking in. Her nails dig in and scratch me as she flails in my arms. She kicks out, hitting the banister and knocking me backward into the wall of the stairwell.

I grip her tighter, shaking her slightly and pinning her small body still between me and the wall. "Stop!" I scream at her. She whimpers, cowering as her tears trail down her face and soak into my shirt.

It fucking destroys me that she knows. I'll fix this. I don't have any other choice but to make this right. I can't let her go.

Her shoulders shake as I take another two steps up before she's at it again.

This doesn't change a damn thing... Jules is still mine.

To be continued...

ALTHOUGH JULES and Mason got their happily ever after under

false pretenses, it could never have lasted. Mason should have known that from the start, and in many ways he did. The truth always comes out, and when it does, everything changes and a new story begins.

UNFORGIVEN, the conclusion of the duet, is available now!

ABOUT WILLOW

Thank you so much for reading my romances. I'm just a stay at home mom and avid reader turned author and I couldn't be happier.
I hope you love my books as much as I do!

More by Willow Winters
www.willowwinterswrites.com/books/

READING ORDER

Standalone Novels:
Broken
Forget Me Not
Little Liar
Possessive
Forsaken, cowritten with B. B. Hamel
Burned Promises

Sins and Secrets Duets:
Imperfect (Imperfect Duet book 1)
Unforgiven (Imperfect Duet book 2)

Damaged (Damaged Duet book 1)
Scarred (Damaged Duet book 2)

Valetti Crime Family Series:
Dirty Dom
His Hostage
Rough Touch
Cuffed Kiss

Bad Boy

**Highest Bidder Series,
cowritten with Lauren Landish:**
Bought
Sold
Owned
Given

**Bad Boy Standalones,
cowritten with Lauren Landish:**
Inked
Tempted
Mr. CEO

**On the Sweeter Side,
cowritten with Vivian Wood:**
Knocking Boots
Promise Me

Happy reading and best wishes,
Willow xx

CPSIA information can be obtained
at www.ICGtesting.com
Printed in the USA
BVHW040353290520
580536BV00018B/295